The Rival Games

'But these aren't the Olympics, are they? They're just, well, a make-believe equivalent. They're just a bit of a laugh, really. That's what –'

'Oh, no they're not!' Kristian cut in fiercely. 'They're nothing of the sort. They've got to be taken seriously. Anyway, if you think they're a joke, why are you out training now?'

MICHAEL HARDCASTLE

The Rival Games

Illustrated by Trevor Parkin

A Magnet Book

First published in Great Britain 1988
by Methuen Children's Books Ltd
This edition first published 1989
by Magnet Paperbacks
A Division of Octopus Group
Michelin House, 81 Fulham Road, London SW3 6RB
Text copyright © 1988 Michael Hardcastle
Illustrations copyright © 1988 Trevor Parkin
Printed in Great Britain
by Cox & Wyman Ltd, Reading

ISBN 0 416 13722 9

Contents

1

Running Into Form

Kristian Meldrum was nerving himself to go headlong into the softest sand when he caught a glimpse of the girl. He'd already done enough hard work for one hot day but five more minutes wouldn't kill him, he decided. If he ploughed through the sand without once coming off his bicycle then he would have achieved more than he'd thought possible. He'd become a record-breaker.

On the other hand, he didn't want to become bogged down in a morass. If he couldn't control the bike then he'd fall off. And look a total idiot. If, that is, the girl was watching him. He couldn't tell what she was doing at the moment so he'd have to sneak a glance in her direction.

She'd not only spotted him, she knew him.

'Hey, Kris, is this where you do your training, then?' she called out as she started to head towards him from the water's edge.

He winced at the shortening of his name. But nobody bothered to listen when he complained.

'Sometimes,' he answered cautiously.

'I'm whacked, absolutely whacked,' she told him, holding her T-shirt away from her chest to allow air to circulate and cool her down. 'I don't know why I do this, I really don't. It's torture. I must be absolutely mad. Bonkers.'

And, just to emphasise the point she was making, she shook her head so vigorously her shoulder-length blonde hair swung across her face like a curtain in a gale.

'Running's *easy* compared to riding a bike through wet sand. That *really* exhausts you. Try it and see.'

Susie Linacre looked suitably appalled by that suggestion. 'You must be mad, too!' she exclaimed before sinking down on to the sand in mock exhaustion. 'But then, you've always been dead keen about everything, haven't you, Kris?'

'Not everything, no. But I am keen to win a gold medal in the Rival Games. I'd like to stand on that podium and be presented with a winner's medal so that everybody in the village knew that I was champion young cyclist for miles and miles around.'

Susie shook her head again, this time in mild disbelief that anyone should cherish such an ambition. 'Even if you get it, that medal won't be real gold, you know,' she pointed out. 'It'll just be gilt at best.'

'That doesn't matter to me,' Kris said rather airily. 'Prizes aren't the important thing. It's competing and coming first, that count. That's the true Olympic spirit.'

'But these aren't the Olympic Games, are they? They're just, well, a sort of make-believe equivalent. They're just a bit of a laugh, really. That's what –'

'Oh no they're not!' Kristian cut in fiercely. 'They're nothing of the sort. They've got to be taken seriously. Anyway, if you think they're a joke why are you out training now?'

For a moment Susie didn't say anything. Instead, she suddenly sank on to the sand, stretching out her long legs and crossing them at the ankles.

'Wish there was a café or something round here, I'm as dry as an old bone,' she announced.

'There'll be some mobile vans along here before long – when the season begins, that is,' Kristian told her.

'Oh, you're a lot of help! I'm dying of thirst now and you tell me if only I can hang on a few weeks there'll be plenty to drink. Thanks a billion!'

She paused and then added wistfully: 'I suppose you haven't got anything to drink in that saddle-bag of yours, have you? I mean, you're always supposed to be organised about everything at school.'

Kristian hoped she wouldn't notice that the saddle-bag was bulging. Besides a water container he was carrying fruit and chocolate bars for energy and a first aid kit in case of emergency. Susie was absolutely right about his being prepared for anything.

'Well, er, I have got a little water – only a little, mind you. You see –'

'Well, come on, then, Kris, share it out! I mean, I'll probably die on the spot, otherwise. Then you'll be to blame because people will find out you were the last person to talk to me and you refused, *refused*, to share your life-saving liquid with me. They may even want to sling you in jail on a girl-slaughter charge!'

Kristian gulped, something he was able to do easily because his mouth wasn't at all dry. 'Look,' he began severely, 'if you go out on long-distance running on a hot day you ought to take something to drink with you. That's common sense. Every runner is in danger of suffering dehydration in these conditions. All the best sports books tell you that sort of thing.'

'I don't need to read books to learn how to run properly! I'm pretty good at it normally. It's just that it's so darned hot today. Come on, Kris, give us a drink. *Please*.'

10

Rather reluctantly he unstrapped the bag and then handed her the plastic container of water. She astonished him by how much she simply poured down her throat and he thought she was going to empty the bottle.

'Thanks,' she said, wiping her lips with the back of her hand. 'I definitely needed that. You're not so bad after all, Kris.'

'Listen,' he said as he retrieved the container, 'you didn't answer my question. Why are you out training if you think the Rival Games are just a joke? Why get yourself all worked up like this for nothing?'

Susie sat up, clasped her legs tightly with her arms and lowered her chin until it was resting on her knees. He began to suspect that she wasn't going to give him an answer and that would be annoying. Kristian didn't care for mysteries. He liked everything in life to be made clear to him.

'Well, you see, it's like this,' she said slowly, drawing out each word as if it were a piece of elastic. 'My friend Lynda Casco thinks these Games are just great. She goes on about them as if they'd been invented just for her benefit. So she's going in for everything. And I'm sick of her boasting about what she's going to win and how far she's going to win by – and all that rubbish. Well, I mean, it may not be rubbish when it happens. I mean, she's not bad at running and jumping and all that sort of stuff. So –'

'But what's that got to do with you?' Kristian cut in impatiently. 'Look, I haven't got all day to listen to you. I've got to get on with my vital training.'

'You sound just like Lynda,' Susie told him, unperturbed by his attitude. 'Anyway, you asked me to tell you and I'm telling you. So just relax, Kris, and listen. I need a rest so I'm having one.'

With a sigh of irritation Kris lowered his bike to the sand and carefully sat down so that he could face Susie. He hadn't known that she and Lynda were friends but that wasn't really sur-prising because they looked so alike and sometimes were mistaken for sisters. Kristian preferred Lynda because whenever she saw him out training she gave him an encouraging smile and said she hoped his times were improving. Lynda plainly took him seriously as an athlete.

'Well, I've had her boasting up to here,' res-umed Susie, placing the edge of her hand against her throat. 'So I decided I'd win some-thing myself. That'll put her in her place. And that's why I'm out training now, OK? Got the idea, Kris?'

He nodded but in a deliberately superior manner. 'Oh yes, I can see what you're after.

But training alone isn't good enough, you know. It won't guarantee that you'll win anything. You've got to have – well, *determination*. You've got to want to win *like mad*.'

'Oh, but I do,' Susie replied calmly. 'I'm determined to beat Lynda at something, and I reckon she hasn't got a lot of stamina. She's all for sprints and short distances. But I can keep going for ever. That's –'

'But you're not properly *organised*,' he interrupted again. 'I told you, if you're going on long runs in the heat you'll suffer dehydration if you don't drink enough. You can be in real danger if you don't prepare properly. Running can be a dangerous sport.'

Susie sat up sharply. 'Listen, have you heard about the javelin? It's awful what happened to Sharon. I always said javelins were dangerous. They ought to have been banned before this.'

Kristian, too, sat up straight. 'No. What's happened? My sister Fiona's going in for the javelin event.'

'Well, she can forget that! It's off. Cancelled. Finito. Somebody was fooling around with a javelin near school last night and Sharon got in the way. Almost pinned her to the ground, it did.'

'What! Is she dead?'

'No, not as bad as that. Sharon's quite tough,

really. She'll get over it. Just a flesh wound, somebody said. Oh, and lots of bruises. And shock. But it scared lots of people so they've decided javelins are off.'

'My sister will be *devastated*,' Kris declared, awe-struck. 'She's been practising like mad and everyone thought she was going to win.' He paused and then added. 'Well, *some* people did, the ones that Fiona had told she was going to be the best.'

'Well, there are plenty of other events for her

to go in for, aren't there? You and she could enter for the three-legged race and –'

'Oh no we couldn't!' Kristian exploded. 'You're supposed to take these games seriously. They're not a joke.'

'They're supposed to be *fun*,' Susie pointed out. 'That's the whole idea – it says so in the village Newsletter. The exact words are: "The Rival Games are designed to provide fun and enjoyment for every person in the village." I know that because my uncle is the editor. He wrote that sentence one evening at our house when he called to ask my dad for his opinion. So, of course, I gave him mine, too. Oh yes, and another thing: my cousin Rosalind goes to a school where they still do three-legged races in her year and she's sixteen! Mind you, that's boarding school and funny things go on there from what I hear.'

Kristian hadn't really been listening. 'But the games *are* serious,' he insisted. 'They are being held to honour the memory of the most famous athlete ever born in Amerton Rival. The most famous person of any kind, actually. They commemorate – well, I think that's what they call it – they're to commemorate his wonderful feat in the Olympic Games sixty years ago. So you can't make a *joke* of that. That would be, well, *disgusting*. Like drawing a black beard on his portrait in the Village Hall. Or giving him a moustache or a bald head.'

'Yes, we all know that, Kris, we've all had it drummed into us every blooming year since we were born, I should think. Our Peter Gateway is a bigger hero than anyone who ever lived if you listen to any *old* person in our village. Honestly, you'd think he was more important than the Prime Minister and the Archbishop of Canterbury and – and the top pop singer of the day all rolled into one!'

Kris laughed, which was a rarity. 'Well, they don't call him Saint Peter for nothing, you know!'

'Oh, I do know, don't I just! Saint Peter the Great, hallelujah! The Gateway to Heaven and all that. Anyway, listen. It's time I got going. Don't want to be late for tea. Running makes me feel ravenous. Honestly, I'm absolutely starving already.'

Susie got to her feet and then, very carefully, brushed every grain of sand off her legs and thighs. Aware that Kristian was watching she remarked nonchalantly: 'Might as well make sure that any bit of me that can get brown gets a chance. You never know how long this sunny spell will last.'

Kristian experienced a sudden flash of insight. 'Hey, that's why you come out running, isn't it? Just to get a tan? It's why you wear such short shorts and hardly anything else.'

'Course not!' Susie protested immediately. 'If I just wanted to sunbathe I could stay at home and laze about in the garden or go and find a sun-trap up on the Downs. I told you, I want to beat Lynda at something to put us on level terms. If I get a bit of a tan at the same time, well, that's just a bonus. And I'll tell you another thing, Kristian Meldrum: I sometimes get a stitch, a really bad one, right here under my ribs, but I don't let that stop me running, do I? I just keep going – well, when the pain's eased off I do.'

He didn't think her explanation was particularly convincing but he didn't want to bother arguing. He'd wasted enough time talking to her when he should be concentrating on his training.

'Well, if you get a stitch it's probably because you eat too much before you start running,' he told her dismissively. 'You shouldn't eat *anything* for two or three hours before setting out. All the best guides tell you that if you look.'

'Thanks for nothing,' she replied spiritedly. 'But I didn't eat for two whole *hours* before I set off. And that's why I'm starving now, OK?'

Kristian, who was also now on his feet and picking up his cycle, just shrugged. 'Please

17

yourself. But I'll tell you something else: you're clenching your fists now. Well, you shouldn't do that in a race or when you're running. The manual says it can cause tension in the upper arms and stops your arms swinging freely when you're on the move. You could carry a stone though. That's supposed to be good for you. But not a big stone, just a medium-size pebble. See you!'

On that confident note he hopped neatly on to his bike and pedalled away at his fastest speed. That, he exulted, ought to tell Susie Linacre that he knew exactly what he was talking about when it came to training for athletics.

'Big head!' retorted Susie, though not quite loud enough for Kristian to catch the words. What she really wished was that she had a pebble in her hand to chuck at him.

Then, as she built up her speed into a fast jog, it suddenly occurred to her that she was quite a good cyclist herself. So far as she knew there was nothing to stop her from entering the cycling event in the Rival Games – entering and winning it. Winning it and therefore defeating Kristian Meldrum. That would show him he wasn't nearly as smart as he thought he was.

Then she smiled as yet another clever thought struck her: bike riding was another way of showing off a girl's shapely legs. Susie had no doubt at all that she was an easy winner in that category.

'I suppose these Games are right up your street,' Mrs Aileen Meldrum commented to the owner of the Village Storehouse as she added a jar of Peruvian honey to the long list of foodstuffs she was buying.

'How do you make that out, Mrs Meldrum?' Francis Exley inquired politely. It had always been his policy never to enter into any argument with a customer whatever his personal feelings.

'Well, it's obvious, isn't it? All these extras I have to keep buying to keep Kristian and Fiona happy – and fit, so they claim. If it isn't Peruvian honey it's Hungarian beans or Greek salads or something totally foreign. Costing a fortune, they are.'

'Well, I'm sure they're really good for young, growing bodies,' was the diplomatic view of Mr Storehouse, as everyone in Amerton Rival tended to describe the man who had the best-stocked shop for miles around.

'Good for profits, that's what I'm thinking,' said Mrs Meldrum, a trifle sourly, as she rooted in her multi-pocketed purse for another pound coin or two. 'And I expect you'll be coining it, too, when these blessed Games are

19

actually taking place if all those visitors the Committee are expecting turn up.'

Mr Exley sighed as silently as he could manage, although the sound didn't escape Mrs Meldrum's microphone-sensitive ears.

'The Storehouse *is* making a major financial contribution to the cost of putting on the Games, Mrs Meldrum. We feel – my wife and I – that it's only right that the village's most prestigious store should help pay for the most important event to be held here for, well, they say it must be over fifty years.'

'And I hope it'll be the last for *another* fifty years!' Mrs Meldrum exclaimed, just as Mr Exley was predicting such an answer.

'Oh, Mrs Meldrum, please try and *enjoy* our great festival,' he said earnestly. 'I'm sure it's going to give everyone here a great deal of pleasure, especially the young ones like Kristian and Fiona. You'll be very proud of them if they win medals for finishing first in whatever they're competing for. I know they'll be thrilled because I can tell they're very keen types.'

'Too keen by half,' Mrs Meldrum muttered. 'Wanting all these extras from places I've hardly heard of. They seem to be scouring the whole world just to find the most expensive items. I wish I knew who was putting them up to it.'

'Well, I'm sure of one thing,' the storekeeper

put in hurriedly. 'These Games will really put *us* on the map. Amerton Rival will become the most famous village in the whole of Britain – well, perhaps in Europe as well.'

'Oh, I expect we'll be famous all right in Peru – just because they have to keep increasing their export orders for honey for our Kristian!' said Mrs Meldrum, departing on what she regarded as a triumphant note.

2

Elin's Secret

'I'm in the mood to try anything!' Kerry Embleton announced.

'You don't need to tell me that,' Elin Drayton replied. 'I always know what mood you're in. So I can tell you'll do anything. But, Kerry, just think: if you don't make it you could – well, you could *drown!*'

'No, I couldn't, Elin. Don't be daft. The stream's not deep enough for that, not by a mile.'

Together the girls surveyed the tumbling stream that for so long had been their favourite feature of the woodland on the slopes of the hills above Amerton Rival. They were standing at a point directly opposite what Kerry, in a gush of enthusiasm some time before, had called 'the jumping stones'. Of course, as she told her friends in the village, it wasn't the stones that jumped: they were simply the landing places for anyone clever enough, or rash enough, to attempt to cross the stream in just two strides (or jumps). Trouble was, you had to land at speed, ready to take off again instantly, because otherwise you would be stranded in the middle of the water. A pool had formed on either side of the flat stones and no one knew how deep the water was there. Susie Linacre claimed to have dived into the nearer pool and not even been able to reach the bottom. That story was usually discounted because it was recognised that Susie had a vivid imagination but a lack of truthful recall, as one of her teachers expressed it.

'Just because nobody we know has actually drowned doesn't mean it's impossible,' Elin persisted. She was quite small for her age and didn't have a reputation for being very adventurous. Her eyes were as dark as the depths of the pool and she worried constantly about her friends and her family.

Kerry began jumping on the bank, her mane of dark, wavy hair bouncing rhythmically on her shoulders. 'I'm sure I can do it, I'm sure I can,' she said fervently. 'You know I've got big feet, so that's a help. Even if I don't land right in the middle of the stone I'll be all right: I won't slip off with my great feet. You know, it's going to be a bit like a hop, a step and a jump. Remember when we played that when we were tinies?'

'Kerry, this isn't a game any more,' Elin pointed out deflatingly. 'It could be, well, it could be a matter of life and death. I mean, just look at the waterfall. See how much water is pouring down. I know it's quite calm when it gets to here but that's because it's *deep*, deep, deep down there, down in that pool.'

'Oh, Elin, why do you always have to look on the black side of everything? Look, these Games are supposed to be loads of fun. They're to make everyone cheerful and happy. Not *gloomy*. That's why I'm going in for the long jump. When I win that I *will* be happy.'

'You won't win anything if you drown yourself, will you? You've got to be sensible, Kerry, and take care. Come on, let's get back home. There's that serial on the telly, the one about that girl who was an orphan when Queen Victoria was a little girl more than a hundred years ago and she had to work in a factory that made –'

'Oh, who cares, who cares about television!' Kerry shouted. She shouted so loud that birds took off from nearby trees in panic. 'Who wants to watch telly when you can actually do exciting things for real like jumping across a dangerous stream! Only you, Elin, only you. But not me. I'm going to jump. No danger.'

Purposefully she marched back from the bank in measured style, trying to work out how many paces she should take before she struck the jumping-off point. In athletics, she believed, you had to plan carefully. Every centimetre counted in a long jump.

'Kerry, wait a second!' Elin pleaded. 'What if you *do* miss the stones and fall in the pool? What about your clothes?'

'They'll get wet, like me. So what? But I'm *not going to miss the stones*. I'm going to get a record that may never be beaten. After what I've done I'll be the most famous female athlete in the village. Nobody'll bother trying to challenge me for the long jump title. I'll get a walk-over and –'

'Please *listen*, Kerry. If you fall in your clothes will be soaked. So how're you going to get home then?'

That made her confident friend stop and consider; but only for a moment. 'I'll just have to strip off then, won't I?'

'Kerry! You can't do that here! It'd –'

'Why ever not? Nobody's going to see me, nobody comes nosing round here, not at this time of day, anyway.'

Elin, of course, thought otherwise. 'You never know, Kerry. It's just the sort of thing that *would* happen, somebody turning up just when you don't want them to. My mum says life's always like that. "The worst thing happens just when it's not wanted." She always says that.'

'She would,' Kerry muttered under her

breath, but not loud enough for Elin to hear. Elin had enough troubles to bear in life, in Kerry's opinion, without anyone topping them up with unkind remarks. 'Look, Elin, I'm determined to have a go at this now. I said I was in the mood, and I am. So you just keep watch and yell like mad if you see anyone coming in this direction. OK?'

Kerry slipped out of her jeans. Elin was beginning to make her uncharacteristically nervous. Sometimes she wondered why she spend so much time in the company of the intense, sad-eyed girl. But it was hard to reject someone who admired you so much.

Elin planted herself beside a spindly birch as a prime look-out point but all her real attention was on Kerry, now measuring out her approach run. She was obviously too interested in what she was doing to be at all self-conscious in her brief attire.

'Go on, Kerry, go on! You can do it!' she urged under her breath. She desperately wanted her friend to succeed; if she managed this jump then it would boost her confidence sky-high for the real thing at the Rival Games. Elin believed she herself would never be good at anything – apart, perhaps, from being a friend – but she felt she could share in Kerry's triumph.

Kerry wasn't particularly tall but she had

strength in her legs, strength that would give her the spring she needed to clear the first obstacle, strength that might enable her to bound on across the second stretch of water. Elin guessed it would be a close thing.

As Kerry made a trial run Elin hastily surveyed the approaches to their arbour. Through a gap that faced south she could just make out the spire of the village church and, by craning her head a little, even the parapet of the tower. It was, as she and other children had been told numberless times, exceedingly rare for a church to possess both tower and spire; but then Amerton Rival had always been one up on its neighbouring villages and especially Amerton Magna. That was why Amerton Magna adopted a very snooty attitude to its twin: it simply ignored anything to do with Amerton Rival, treating it as if it didn't even exist.

No one was to be seen, not even in the far distance, and the only sounds were those of chattering birds. Elin was relieved.

Now Elin's attention was entirely on her friend as those muscular legs carried Kerry at accelerating speed towards the selected take-off point. 'You'll make it, Kerry, you'll make it!' Elin told herself.

Then, just when it seemed she must begin her awesome leap, Kerry suddenly veered sideways

27

and stumbled in some ancient bracken as she tried to pull herself up.

'What's wrong, Kerry, what's wrong?' Ellen yelled in dismay. 'Oh, you haven't hurt yourself, have you?'

'Course I haven't!' Kerry exploded fiercely, pulling herself to her feet. 'I just got the measuring wrong, that's all. Was going to take off half a stride too soon, or too late. That's *fatal*. But I'll get it right this time.'

She turned confidently at the end of her walk-back and, without breaking stride, began to power towards the stream. In spite of her promise to act as look-out Elin couldn't take her eyes off her friend. Kerry raced towards the take-off point and, this time, sprang into the air.

She cleared the first channel with ease, landing on the flat stone with her left foot and then, almost instantaneously, pushing off with her right. Elin felt like applauding. But, of course, Kerry was only half-way to achieving her aim. And although she made a valiant effort to reach the far shore she couldn't quite manage it. Her toes just touched the shallow bank but her balance was wrong: she was falling backwards, not forwards. Despairingly she threw out her arms to try and grasp a sturdy bush that was growing out of the bank. She missed it by millimetres. With a cry of anger rather than

28

anguish she slipped into the water which promptly covered her to the waist.

'Oh, Kerry, are you all right?' Elin wailed, rushing to her friend's aid.

She was, of course, on the wrong bank to be able to offer practical assistance. But any request for help would have had Elin plunging into the stream to rescue her.

'Of course I am!' Kerry declared furiously, hauling herself on to the bank. 'All I've done is get a bit damp and that'll soon dry out. I'm just mad I didn't get all the way across. I was so, so near!'

'You're sure you haven't injured yourself?'

'I told you I haven't! For heaven's sake, Elin, don't I look all right?'

'Yes, but –'

'Well then, stop wittering! The only thing that's wrong with me is that I didn't get all the way across. But I will next time.'

Elin was still anxious. 'But, Kerry, how're you going to get back to this side? I mean, you can't get a proper run from there to jump because of the trees.'

'Well, I've got two alternatives. One, I could swim across if the water's too deep in the pool, or wade if it isn't. Two, I could stay on this side and just run down to where the woods end at the boundary wall. The stream goes underground there, right under the wall, so no problem. I think that's my best bet.'

'But what about your jeans? You can't go around wearing, well, just panties!'

'Course I can! Look, sports shorts for girls these days are no bigger than panties, are they? So who's going to notice the difference? Just supposing, that is, anyone turns up? They'll just think I'm a jogger.' She grinned at the sight of Elin's tortured expression. 'Anyway, I'll dry off quicker if I'm not wearing jeans. Right, I'm going. See you down at the wall, Elin. And don't forget to take my jeans with you.'

There was no likelihood of Elin making that mistake. Bundling them under her arm she had to sprint as she'd never sprinted before to keep Kerry in sight on the opposite bank. All the time she was plunging through thick under-growth or skirting trees she was worrying that someone would see. But no one did. The wood was as deserted as Kerry had forecast it would be.

They were reunited at the drystone wall with Elin feeling quite exhausted by her exertions even though Kerry had to wait for her to catch up. Silently the jeans were handed over and Kerry put them on.

'I'm more or less dry now so I might as well wear them,' she remarked as if she'd had a difficult decision to make. 'You feeling OK, Elin?'

'Yes, of course. Why shouldn't I be?'

Kerry shrugged. 'It's just that you look a bit, well, miserable, down in the dumps, sort of.'

'All *I* was worried about was somebody seeing you in that state,' Elin replied primly. 'It wouldn't have taken long for the news to have spread all through the village, you know. Nobody in Rival can keep a secret for five minutes!'

'That's what you think!' Kerry responded with a gurgling laugh. 'I can think of a few secrets not a soul knows about except me. Oh, and the other person, too.'

Elin stared at her friend. 'Such as?' she asked.

'Well, naturally, I can't tell you, can I? Cos if I did it wouldn't be a secret anymore, would it?'

'But I'm supposed to be your best friend,' Elin pointed out, her lips beginning to tremble a trifle. 'You said so yourself the other week.'

'Maybe I did,' Kerry conceded. 'But there are some things a girl doesn't share even with her best friend. Sorry, Elin.'

A few moments later Elin announced in a quiet voice: 'Well, I've got a secret of my own. But I'd like to share it with you.'

Kerry was delighted by this unexpected offer. 'Oh sure, Elin! Come on, then, tell: what is it?'

'It's at home. I'll have to show you there.'

'Right! Let's hurry then. Come on, let's *run*.'

That wasn't at all what Elin wanted but she had no option but to follow in Kerry's slipstream as her friend broke into a fast run. Elin's home was on the outskirts of the village and it always seemed to Kerry to be much too cramped for such a large family. Although Elin had several brothers and sisters she always insisted she didn't really get on with any of them; she'd confessed to Kerry she quite often felt lonely.

'But you always have people around you so how can you feel lonely?' Kerry asked in disbelief.

'There's nobody of my age so nobody understands just how I feel,' was the reply.

True enough, Kerry admitted, Elin seemed to be right in the middle with three brothers three or more years older than her and three sisters three or or more years younger than her. It was, Kerry recognised, a rather odd family.

Only one of her sisters was to be seen when Elin arrived home, quite breathless, and so no one intercepted them as they darted up the stairs to the bedroom she shared with her eldest sister. She sidled past the nearer of the twin beds and then pointed to a glass-fronted box that appeared to be stuffed with straw or some peculiar-coloured fronds on a layer of peat.

'He's in there!' she announced in a hushed voice, her eyes widening as she spoke.

'Who is? Oh, is it a hamster? Oh, how cute, Elin. Is he allowed out? Can I touch him?'

Kerry wasn't especially keen on furry rodents but she didn't want to disappoint her friend by her reaction. Elin hadn't much in life to get excited about.

'Yes, of course he's allowed out. I handle him every day, many times. He knows me better than, than his mother. Well, I suppose I am his mother in a way. He just loves me, don't you, Hoover?'

Kerry had been on the point of saying something to divert this rather sickly mush that Elin was wallowing in; but the name stopped her.

'*Hoover*? Is that what you call it? What sort of name is that, Elin?'

'Very appropriate. He's called that because he simply makes everything you put in front of him disappear! That's right, isn't it, Hoovie darling?'

'Does he do anything apart from eat?' asked Kerry, trying not to wince.

'He certainly does! He's an artist, an athlete. Actually, he's just amazing.'

Kerry couldn't suppress a sigh. 'Doing what, for instance?'

'Driving his own spaceship, that's what.' Sounding very, very smug.

This was beyond belief. This time Kerry's expression showed.

'Well, I'll just *show* you,' Elin said fiercely.

She dived into a wardrobe and emerged with a transparent plastic ball somewhat larger in diameter than a tennis ball. Deftly she separated the halves which joined together and then went to collect the hamster.

'Come on, Hoover,' she said encouragingly. 'Show us your party trick, clever boy.'

The hamster displayed no unwillingness to

enter the plastic ball and, as soon as the halves were joined again, Elin placed it on the floor. Instantaneously it was on the move as the hamster, working his legs furiously as if he were on a treadmill, propelled it forward. The ball inevitably collided with a bed leg but Hoover almost literally took that in his stride. Simply by shifting his weight a fraction he set the ball rolling again, this time in a different direction. And so it went on: every time the ball struck an obstacle the animal turned it in another direction and kept it moving at a very impressive speed.

'Fantastic!' breathed Kerry, totally impressed by this phenomenon. 'But did you teach him to do that?'

'Oh, it wasn't hard, really,' Elin said modestly. 'He took to it straight away. He enjoys every single moment in his space capsule.'

'I can see that,' Kerry agreed, watching with admiration as Hoover now negotiated a rather tricky turn by a low table that separated the beds. 'He must use up an awful lot of energy: his little legs are going like the clappers. Doesn't he get, well, exhausted?'

'Oh no, he'd stay in there all day if I'd let him. Never knows when to give up, doesn't Hoovie. He *is* marvellous, isn't he? I knew you'd like him.'

'You really ought to put him on show – you know, like a circus performer,' Kerry recommended. 'I'm sure people would pay good money to see something as amazing as that.'

Elin smiled a quite brilliant smile for her. 'I'm glad you said that, Kerry. You see, I was thinking that he ought to take part in the Rival Games.'

Momentarily, Kerry was flabbergasted. 'But there isn't an – an obstacle race for animals,' she pointed out.

'I know, but there ought to be, oughtn't there? I mean, why shouldn't they have special events for pets? Many people in Rival have pets. So I think there ought to be something specially for them. Then Hoover could win a medal. A gold, probably. I think I might get a mention, too, as his owner and trainer. What do you think, Kerry?'

'Well, it's a thought,' Kerry replied, not knowing what else to say because she could tell Elin was being perfectly serious. 'It's definitely a thought.'

3

Any Other Business?

The Amerton Rival Games Committee met in a back room at the Black Bull public house on the Green just as often as C.R. Judge, the Chairman, could get everybody together for an official meeting. Meetings of any kind were his passion; and, because he was quite famous in his way, he invariably expected to be in charge, to be Chairman. His fame owed everything to cricket and umpiring: so his name was known even in places like Allahabad in India and Wellington in New Zealand.

One person who wasn't particularly impressed by C.R. Judge was Kirk Heaton, a former all-round sportsman and now landlord of the Black Bull. Once, years ago, Mr Judge refused to give a player out, caught at the wicket, when Kirk Heaton was the bowler. If his appeal had been successful then Kirk would have achieved the first hat trick of his career; and, as things turned out, it would also have been the *only* hat trick of his career. That incident still rankled. What's more, Kirk felt strongly that he himself should be Chairman of the Games Committee. After all, the meetings were held in his pub where he liked to feel he was completely in charge.

At every meeting there was a lot to get through and Mr Judge had called for an early start that Sunday. Naturally, it wasn't a time that suited Kirk. As usual, the pub had been exceedingly busy the previous night and he'd had little enough sleep. Mr Judge, who didn't drink in pubs and habitually was in bed before 10 pm, wasted no time in calling everyone to order. Wearing one of his favourite cricket souvenirs, a silver-buttoned blazer in black-and-green stripes, he frowned at Mr Heaton who, in his opinion, looked half-asleep as well as half-dressed.

'Are you with us this morning, Mr Heaton?' he inquired coolly.

Kirk sat up, looked round the room, peering pointedly into every corner, and then languidly turned back to look at Mr Judge. 'I don't *seem* to be missing anywhere, Mr Chairman,' he said with an air of puzzled politeness.

Mr Judge sniffed as if he'd just started a cold. He could tell he was going to have a difficult morning with young Heaton, always a trouble-maker. But he wasn't going to let that worry him. In his time, C.R. Judge had dealt with explosive England fast bowlers and ferocious Australian cricket captains and he didn't regard young Heaton as the equal of them in any way.

'Perhaps,' he said, smiling genially at everyone else, 'we can begin. There's a lot on the agenda, as you see. So let's get on with the first item: a replacement for the javelin event. Personally, as you know, I'm not sorry about the loss of this so-called sport because it always struck me as highly dangerous. So do we have any suggestions, ladies and gentlemen?'

'I don't know, Mr Chairman, that we were right to abandon the javelin,' Kirk put in quickly. 'I mean, you can't stop kids fooling about, can you? Kids have always done that; it's what makes 'em so likeable. And Sharon herself wasn't hurt, not really. Shaken a bit, yes. But she's a big, tough lass and can take care of herself. She'd been throwing the javelin herself, you know, before –'

'I asked for suggestions, Mr Heaton,' the Chairman said coldly, 'not a post-mortem. Do you have a positive suggestion to make? If not, you're wasting the Committee's time.'

'My suggestion, *Mr Chairman*, is that we stick to the javelin. We shouldn't chuck the javelin away, if you see what I mean. It's one of our most traditional sports, based on the days when folk threw spears to get their dinners.'

One or two members laughed aloud at the indended pun and others smiled; Kirk could be quite funny when he was in good form. Mr Judge, of course, wasn't in the mood for humorous comments. Committee work was serious business and should be treated accordingly. His next sniff was loud enough to be heard outside the room.

'You are overlooking the fact that the sub-committee on Events has already taken the decision to delete the javelin. Nobody else objected to that. So it is now a *fact* that it has been excluded. I say again, we have no time to waste on matters already determined. Now. . . .'

He looked round inquiringly and then focused on Miss Serena Selby, Head of the local school, whom he regarded as one of his supporters. He was taken with her blue eyes and gentle voice; and he was also aware that she was a strict disciplinarian in her profession. She wasn't, as he thought of it, 'soft with children and forever giving in to them.' But Miss Selby was saying nothing for the present. She quite liked Kirk Heaton and she especially liked his reference to children being likeable. His view rather surprised her because he wasn't married and he hadn't any children of his own. He often spoke a lot of sense, she believed. Mr Judge, she suspected, didn't care for children as much as he claimed he did.

'Right, we'll move on, then,' the Chairman said briskly, confident he had overcome the opposition yet again. 'So now we have to decide what should replace the javelin. I believe we have a suggestion from our youngest committee member.'

He smiled benignly at Hannah Donini, who was still at school where she was, in fact, the most popular pupil, not least because her father's firm manufactured ice-cream that even people in Amerton Magna described as scrumptious. Indeed, it had an international reputation, for tourists from as far away as Rome and Madrid still returned home to rave about Donini Delicious.

'Well, we think – the children, I mean – that we ought to have a football-throwing contest,' said Hannah, giving a characteristic flick to her neatly-tied pony tail as she started to speak. 'It's something both girls and boys can do. But the boys really like it.'

'Good, good', said the Chairman encouragingly. 'We always need activities to attract boys. Don't want them sitting on the sidelines. That would never do.'

'But doesn't football just attract the hooligan element?' asked one of the older Committee members with a worried expression.

'Oh, no, not *this* sort of football,' the Chairman said soothingly. 'Perhaps you would explain what this game entails, Hannah.'

'Well, it's quite easy, really. Anyone of any age can play. Take part, I mean. You have to sit on the ground, cross-legged. Oh, and keep behind a special line. And you have got to stay seated. No lifting of, er, of, er, your bottom.'

Kirk Heaton laughed at that, which drew a sharp, reproving look from Mr Judge, but other Committee members just smiled. In any case, they could tell that Hannah wasn't in the slightest embarrassed by the mention of bottom.

'Well, we – sorry, everybody – throws the football – oh yes, you're holding a football as you sit there. You throw it as far as you can and the winner is the one who sends it furthest. And that's all there is to it.'

'Thank you, Hannah,' said the Chairman gravely. 'Any questions?'

'It does sound rather simple,' observed a young housewife, Mrs Kenton. 'But won't it just be won by mad-keen footballers?'

'Oh no!' Hannah exclaimed. 'Some footballers aren't any good at all at using their *hands*. They can only kick well. We've tried out this game at school and some of the girls are really terrific. They make some of the boys look hopeless.'

'Oh, well, we can't object to that then, can we?' murmured Mrs Kenton, and was rather surprised when that comment was greeted with laughter.

Miss Selby gave Hannah an approving nod. She hoped Hannah wasn't going to waste her life by just going into the ice-cream business; the girl was far too intelligent for that. The Head hadn't known what the children were up to when they were asked to devise something to replace the javelin. She liked them to reach their own decisions. What she could have guessed was that Hannah would be the one chosen by the majority of the children to represent them on the Games Committee.

Item by item the Committee worked through the agenda, dealing with such vital matters as. . . . Refreshments: 'If we can persuade old Mrs Middleton to make a couple of extra trays of her famous sausage rolls nobody will go away hungry!' Publicity: 'but I don't see why television shouldn't be asked to cover our Games,' someone argued. 'After all, we all pay our licence fees and they should be the servants of the public.' Competitors' attire: 'We can't have them wearing those really short shorts, they're practically indecent,' the Chairman stated. Car parking: 'We'll have to put up a special notice outside Mr Watson's – he becomes a raving lunatic if anyone parks anywhere near his house.' And fund-raising: 'Who could possibly object to paying a few pence in a raffle to have a chance of winning something *big*?!'

With everyone giving hints about wanting to get away to their Sunday lunch by looking meaningfully at wristwatches, the Chairman conceded that it was about time the meeting was drawing to a close. It was always a disappointment to him when he had to close a meeting so he delayed the moment as long as possible. Today he had what he regarded as a good excuse for prolonging matters.

'Right, ladies and gentlemen, we now reach item 14: Any Other Business. Has anyone anything they wish to raise?'

'Only a hammer, over your head,' Kirk Heaton muttered, well aware that his words would carry to the Chairman. Miss Selby half-smiled and then gave Kirk a warning frown. Hannah very skilfully just prevented herself from giggling. She, too, liked Mr Heaton's boyish manner.

Nobody said anything aloud; and only two people rose from their seats in anticipation of the welcome words from the Chairman, 'I now declare the meeting closed'. But Mr Judge smiled blandly and lifted his hands from the table with a gesture that might have meant 'calm down' but which was actually intended to indicate that he wasn't finished yet.

'Then there is one small point I must raise,' he said to a chorus of silent groans. 'I have received a letter. . . .'

'From someone demanding your resignation?' Kirk asked with unforced cheerfulness.

Miss Selby shot him another warning glance, Hannah had greater difficulty this time suppressing a giggle and Mr Judge himself didn't even deign to glance in Kirk's direction.

'The letter,' he continued coolly, 'is from a young lady called Elin Drayton. It's a very interesting letter, too. She makes the tolerable suggestion that the Rival Games should include something for animals. 'So –'

'*Animals*?' someone inquired with such intense disbelief even Mr Judge blinked.

'Giraffes and rhinos and that sort of thing?' Mr Heaton asked facetiously.

'But the Olympic Games don't go in for dogs and cats and, and *novelties*,' another pointed out.

'If you'll *allow* me,' the Chairman cut in, knowing that everyone would allow him to say

anything he liked – except Mr Heaton, of course. 'What Miss Drayton – er, by the way, do you know her, Miss Selby?'

'One of my pupils,' was the reply. 'Quite an interesting girl, though she doesn't normally say much.'

'She just spends all her time admiring Kerry Embleton,' supplied Hannah, who thought Elin was really very dull indeed.

'Yes, well, if I can get back to her letter,' the Chairman continued, 'I should explain that Elin feels the Games are such a very special occasion in the life of the village that it would be, well, quite wrong to exclude pets from the proceedings – that's my word, by the way, proceedings. But I was giving you the gist of the girl's letter. Does anybody have a positive, a *constructive*, view of the matter?'

He was, of course, hoping to deter Mr Heaton from making any more nonsensical remarks. He failed.

'I suppose we could advertise for a circus to bring along their lions and then they could have a go at our Christians, couldn't they?' Kirk said rather heavily. 'I mean, that's what used to go on at Games in the old days, isn't it? It'd also be useful publicity for our vicar – you know, if the Christians actually won!'

'Really, Mr Heaton, that's not worthy of

you,' Miss Selby chided him while the Chairman looked thunderous. 'And, anyway, you're mixing things up: the lions v the Christians was in the days of the Roman Empire.'

'Oh, sorry – history was never my strong point,' Kirk conceded graciously. Suddenly he realised what a lovely shade of blue Miss Selby's eyes were. It surprised him he'd not noticed that before.

'I suppose we could have a parade of family pets,' Mrs Kenton said, 'and award a rosette for the best-behaved, or best-looking or something. Then nobody'd be left out.'

'But how do you choose between dogs and cats, or even just different breeds of dogs, if it comes to that?' someone wanted to know.

'They manage all right at Cruft's,' Mrs Kenton answered smartly.

'It seems,' the Chairman put in with a hint of a grin, 'that we would have more than dogs and cats to consider. Young Elin's pet is a hamster. I don't know whether we could get that creature to parade, could we?'

'I propose, Mr Chairman, that we raise this matter at the next Committee meeting,' suggested the member most anxious to get to his lunch.

'Quite right!' agreed the Chairman to everyone's surprise. 'I think the very best thing is to set up a sub-committee to look into the whole idea. I'm perfectly willing to chair it and I propose that the other two members be Miss Selby and, er, young Hannah. How about it, ladies?'

'Oh, yes, fine,' Miss Selby consented, much to her own surprise.

'Oh, sure, thanks,' said Hannah, pleased as well as surprised to be asked to sit on another committee.

'Very well, then,' said the Chairman, relieved that that had gone so smoothly. 'I now declare the meeting closed.'

'I'll serve on the sub-committee if you like,' Kirk volunteered suddenly. 'I mean, I've got pets of my own.'

'Too late for that,' the Chairman told him promptly. 'The meeting has already been declared closed.'

And he went off smiling genially and thinking he'd treat his own Afghan hound to a romp on the hills. He deserved a reward. Of course, Mr Judge wasn't thinking of the hound when he thought that.

4

Larry Bites Back

 As he swung his bike into Appletree Row, Kristian groaned aloud. 'Oh no! Not that blooming bulldog! Larry, come here, boy. Here boy!'

But Larry, the Meldrums' labrador, took not the slightest notice. He was about to investigate a rubbish pile beside a farmer's gate. Larry adored rubbish.

Kristian had been hoping to avoid any need to get off his bike on this outing. He had thoroughly convinced himself that any moment spent out of the saddle was a moment wasted in his campaign to be regarded as Amerton Rival's top cyclist of all time. This was another vital practice ride and he hadn't intended to take Larry. After all, the dog was supposed to be Fiona's responsibility. But his mother had insisted that he take the dog.

'And as you're mad keen on exercise for yourself, you can take Larry with you and give him a work-out. Keep him on the run and get a few pounds off that fat frame. Now, go on, don't argue. Or else. . . .'

Or else, he knew only too well, he'd be forced to carry out some chore he really hated, such as polishing the parquet floor in the dining-room all on his own. Either that or lose his spending money for a week.

'Come here, you *mad* dog!' he hissed at Larry, noting all the while the bulldog's slow and suspicious and decidedly deadly approach. It never raced at an enemy; it stalked it like a cat fancying a mouse. It would, if it set its mind to it, make mincemeat of Larry. Kristian wouldn't mind too much; but his mother would definitely blame Kristian if he went home and announced that the dog was deceased.

The labrador not only ignored its part-owner but was blissfully unaware of the predatory bulldog. Kristian, determined to keep the two apart, executed a neat figure-of-eight, keeping the bike beautifully balanced. By now he believed that he and his bike were one: the entire machine might have been an extension of his own body. He felt it was impossible for the judges to overlook his skills. If there were any justice in the world he would surely receive an award simply for taking part. But he didn't suppose Mr Judge and his fellow judges would see things quite like that.

When, with acute timing and precision, he very nearly shaved the skin off the bulldog's nose with his front wheel, the dog, not surprisingly, growled fiercely. And at last Larry was alerted to the danger. After one startled look at his old enemy he broke into what for him counted as a run but really was not much more than a quickened lumbering action. Belatedly the bulldog decided to give chase but Kristian, working hard on the pedals, again managed to frustrate him by riding criss-cross fashion in front of the animal. He knew he was risking a bite from the bulldog's iron-strong jaws, but he was relying on his own speed of reaction to get him out of trouble. Larry lolloped on up the lane and eventually he, too, was clear of disaster. The bulldog, having, in its own mind, seen off the trespassers, came to a stop at the edge of its own territory and merely barked a valedictory warning not to come back.

'You see, you stupid animal, you always need me to save you from a horrible fate,' Kristian called to the unheeding Larry. 'Just keep away from rubbish heaps in future.'

His chosen route led up the steepest hillside above the village. That, of course, would help to build the muscles in his legs; but, just as plainly, it was quite beyond Larry's powers to keep going.

The lane was narrow and stony with a wide grass verge on both sides. Larry, rarely having ventured so high, knew of no rubbish piles up there and so wasn't prepared to search. He'd had enough. So he sat down, tongue lolling out, and tried to look appealing when Kristian nagged at him. But, unlike Fiona, Kristian didn't respond to blatant dog appeal. Fiercely he prodded the family dog with his front tyre. Larry looked pained.

'Come *on*, we're supposed to be *training*,' Kristian pointed out. 'Mum says we have to, *both* of us.'

With extreme reluctance Larry removed his rump from the grass and waddled a few metres upwards. It was really too steep for Kristian to ride but he wasn't going to let a mere gradient defeat him. The bike tilted and wobbled and slithered and its rider became more exasperated by the minute.

'It's all *your* fault!' he yelled at the long-suffering Larry, aiming a kick in the dog's general direction.

That insult, coupled with the risk of being injured, caused Larry to do what he'd wanted to do all the time: sit down again. Sit and not get up until he was ready to go home for tea and comfort from the loving Fiona. He'd chosen a resting place directly opposite a gateway leading to an attractive, stone-built house called Post Office Cottage. It was a house well-known not just because of the quaintness of the post box in the wall. Its real fame was due almost entirely to the antics of Gregory the goat.

His full name, in fact, was Gregory Bite and the inspiration for that was the film star, Gregory Peck. The goat, however, packed more of a punch than Mr Peck. Usually, the goat was tied up, but on this day he wasn't. He'd managed to bite through yet another plastic-reinforced-with-wire cord. The sound of Kristian's displeasure alerted Gregory like a fire-bell summoning firemen. He came out running, running fast. Larry, surprising himself as well as Kristian by the speed with which he got to his feet to take avoiding action, bared his teeth and started to snarl. He knew he didn't have the strength to run away so all he could do was stand and fight: but fight for his own life, not that of anyone else in the Meldrum family.

Kristian, naturally alarmed by the sight of the charging Gregory, stepped back – and stumbled over his bike. As he tried to regain his balance his left leg swung into Larry – and Larry promptly sank his teeth into it.

The dog had simply taken his bite too soon: he was preparing to repel Gregory. But Kristian didn't have time to think about that. He was in pain and also in dire danger of being damaged further by a demented goat. Actually, Kristian's yell of pain almost deflected Gregory; he didn't expect people to complain so loudly before he made contact with them. So, instead of biting his newest victim, he simply butted him; butted him hard, of course, and in a tender place. Inevitably, Kristian crashed to the ground.

Larry, deciding for once in his life that defence was better than rapid retreat, stayed where he was, snarling quite dramatically at Gregory. If he had to die, he would die fighting. Gregory was unused to such defiance. Normally people, and other animals, simply fled when he attacked. This time he had a dog that wouldn't run and a boy who, because of anger and pain, looked capable of anything. Moreover, the bike lying on the ground didn't look particularly appetising.

So, a trifle disappointedly, Gregory turned and mooched back to his own yard for a snack of plastic and wire. It had already been a busy day because earlier he'd seen off a postman (who, being a stranger on this round, hadn't known of Gregory's existence, his colleagues forgetting to tell him of the risk he was about to run). So the goat felt he deserved some reward. Later on he might enjoy a yard or two of the spare tyre his owner had unwisely left outside the garage.

'You are a stupid, idiotic, lunatic!' Kristian cursed the family dog. 'Just look at what you've

done! It's still bleeding. And I've probably got
typhus from all the germs you carry from all the
rubbish dumps you muck about with.'

Kristian really meant rabies but he wasn't
thinking straight, which was understandable in
the circumstances. Larry, for his part, was
looking anything but sympathetic. He felt
pleased with himself. After all, he'd defended
the family's honour by seeing off a vicious
enemy. If only his mistress, Fiona, had been

57

present she would have lavished kisses on him and, with a bit of luck, a selection of titbits. But he couldn't expect such an ecstatic response from the unpredictable Kristian.

'I don't know how I'm going to ride home with my leg like this,' Kristian muttered as he subjected the wound to another searching examination. 'I mean, you've practically gone through to the bone, you mad dog. I really should go straight to the hospital.'

It wasn't the immediate ride home he was really thinking about. What troubled him was the possibility that the injury was so bad he wouldn't be able to compete in the Rival Games. It was like hearing that the end of the world was nigh. After all the training he'd put in, all the effort he'd made, all –

'Hi, Kris! What're you resting for? I thought you were supposed to be super-fit!'

Susan Linacre, descending the hill at a nice, steady pace so that she wouldn't slip on a sharp stone, had spotted him. Wearing her usual brief attire, she was out on a training run and trying a new route. It was Kristian himself who'd inspired her with the idea of using hills to improve her stamina and performance; but, naturally, she wasn't going to tell him that.

'I've, er, well, had an accident,' Kristian admitted. He'd rather have said nothing but he couldn't ignore her: anyway, she could see for herself he was bleeding.

She slowed to a halt, scenting something interesting. Then she spotted the wound. Her eyes almost lit up. Susie was not exactly bloodthirsty, but injuries and misfortune always interested her. She often thought a career in medicine could be stimulating.

'You haven't been *bitten*, have you?' she inquired with some relish, casting a surprised look at the dog.

'Well, er, not, er, *deliberately*,' Kristian mumbled, uncertain what to admit to. 'It, er, was an accident, you see.'

'Bitten by your *own* dog!' Susie exclaimed. If true, she had a brilliant story to relate at school. 'I didn't know your dog was dangerous. Looks soft, to me.'

'Well, he's not really. Not usually, I mean. But, er, well – oh, it doesn't matter.' Kristian had had enough of explanations. The bite was beginning to sting and he knew he ought to get proper attention. 'Er, look, Susie, do you think you could help a bit and –'

'Sorry! Can't stop now. I'm out on a training run, you see. Should be timing myself really.' What she was thinking about was Kristian's meanness over the water when she was so desperate for a drink on the beach the other day.

Anyway, he had a bike and could ride off for help if he needed it. 'See you,' she called, breaking into an impressive sprint.

'Girls!' Kristian mouthed disgustedly. They were all the same: only thought of themselves. 'Come on, *dog*,' he ordered, picking up his bike. 'We're off home.'

Larry moved with alacrity. The way home was all downhill and his beloved mistress would feed him properly. He had a lot to look forward to. Which was more than could be said for the suffering Kristian. He guessed he wouldn't get any sympathy at all from his family when they learned it was Larry who'd bitten him. Probably they wouldn't even believe it. Perhaps, on reflection, it might be best not to mention the incident at all. But he'd have to find a way of explaining away his terrible injury, the injury that might destroy his sporting career.

Elin was ecstatic.

'Honestly, I didn't think they'd actually send me a letter,' she exclaimed to Kerry Embleton. 'I mean, they could have just, well, ignored it, couldn't they?'

'They could,' said Kerry rather heavily. She was beginning to get a bit fed up with Elin's excitement. 'But I suppose Mr Judge is the sort of man who always does everything by the book

– you know, he has strict rules of conduct. Umpires are like that, my dad says. And he's really old-fashioned – Mr Judge, I mean, not my dad!'

'Well, I think it's wonderful. I mean, they're actually going to do what I suggested. We're going to have an event for *animals* at the Rival Games! Terrific. I mean, listen to this Kerry, listen to what the letter says: "The General Committee likes your suggestion. Accordingly, we have appointed a sub-committee to look into the matter and decide what form the event for animals should take. Thank you again for your suggestion." Isn't that great?'

'*Wonderful*,' agreed Kerry, without trying to disguise the sarcasm. 'Now, Elin could we possibly think of something else. I do have to get on with some serious training today, you know.'

'Oh, well, I suppose so,' said Elin rather dreamily. 'But first I must go and tell Hoovie that his big chance has come – well, I mean, it will come on Games Day. Just imagine, Hoovie, you're going to be a star!'

Kerry raised her eyes to the skies, but not in expectation of seeing what sort of star the hamster might become. What had started as quite a funny idea was turning into serious nonsense, as Kerry thought of it. The Rival Games were intended to be miniature Olympics where *people* performed to the best of their athletic abilities. If assorted animals were allowed to do their thing as well then the whole occasion could become a farce. She was amazed that Mr Judge hadn't realised that and so squashed any idea of introducing pets into the proceedings.

'Oh, come *on*, Elin, you can say all that later,' Kerry said as she irritatedly watched her friend praising Hoovie for his brilliant talents. 'I told you, I *must* train today and I need your support. You can slobber over the hamster when I'm not here.'

Elin grinned as a thought struck her. 'I'm not sure, you know, that you ought not to address me as Miss Drayton. I mean, that's what Mr Judge did. Look at the letter: "Dear Miss Drayton." That's what it says. Not just Elin. You see, Mr Judge is a, a gentleman. He knows how to treat ladies.'

'He's bonkers, and you are as well if that's what you think,' Kerry told her curtly. 'Look, I'm going on my own if you're not coming. I've wasted enough of the morning as it is.'

She marched out of the house without another word.

'Oh, Kerry, wait for me,' Elin wailed, running to catch up.

*

'Do you know,' remarked Mrs Embleton as she emerged from the Village Storehouse with her friend the Vicar, 'nobody in this village meanders any more. They run everywhere. It used to be so quiet here, too. You must remember that, Dylan. It was so quiet you could hear a bee buzz.'

'And now it's like the inside of a hive!' smiled the Vicar, sharing in her simile. He had a fondness for Mrs Embleton he wouldn't admit to anyone.

'And all these advertisements, just look at 'em in the far window,' she went on, pointing back to the Storehouse. 'People wanting to sell running shoes and exercise bikes and dumbbells. The entire village has gone sports mad.'

'Healthy, though, isn't it, Jacqueline? I mean, it's good for the body, for fitness.' He paused and then risked a minor joke. 'Not sure what it does to the spirit.'

'I'll be thankful when it's over,' Mrs Embleton sighed. 'Then life can get back to normal.'

'Oh, I don't know,' admitted the Rev. Dylan K. Jones. 'Some people might find out they're good at things they never suspected. Like, er, long-distance running. Have you never thought you might be good at that? Might it not, er, run in the family?'

'We're not a sporting family at all,' she said flatly. 'Not in any way.'

'Oh.' His hopes of accompanying her on a jog one evening were dashed. 'But surely Kerry has some, er, sporting ambitions, hasn't she?'

'Not likely! All she's interested in is pop music and film actors and discos and money. She wouldn't run a yard if her socks were on fire.'

'Oh,' said the Vicar again, diplomatically this time. He sensed Jacqueline might be surprised on Games Day if what he had seen on his strolls through the woods was to be believed.

5

The Barefoot Jumper

The rain was sparkling on the lawn when Steve Crashley drew aside his bedroom curtains just as the sun was beginning to come up. He uttered an oath, as he liked to describe it if anyone criticised him for swearing. It wasn't one of his mildest curses this time, either. He'd been praying for a dry morning and the fates had let him down. *Again*, he reminded himself.

'But it's not going to stop me,' he muttered. Steve had long had the habit of talking to himself. He believed it was a sign of a determined athlete to keep encouraging himself verbally. A high-jumper was a lonely figure and he needed to hear an encouraging voice: his own. If other competitors thought he was a little crazy, well, that was just their opinion. By jumping higher than anyone else he'd prove he was a champion, and champions could get away with unusual behaviour. All that really counted was being the best.

For a moment he considered getting back into

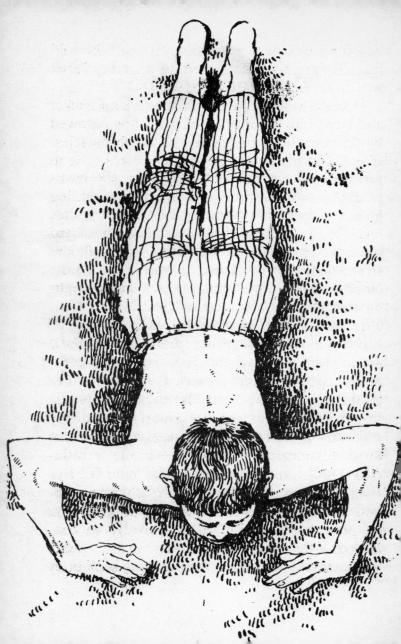

bed for an extra fifteen minutes. 'No!' he told himself fiercely. 'That would be cheating. That won't do. Get on with it, Steve.'

Decisively he stripped off his pyjama jacket and went into his routine of press-ups followed by an exercise to strengthen his thigh muscles. If it hadn't been so early he would have gone in for running on the spot. But the vibrations would carry to his parents' room. The last thing he wanted was to awaken them. A few minutes later he stole down to the kitchen, hesitated before the pantry (a wedge of Cheddar would be so welcome now) and then made his way to the spare land behind the house which was set right on the outskirts of Amerton Rival.

It was there, surrounded by wildly overgrown bushes and other dense vegetation, that he'd established his private training ground. He'd never seen another person there and Steve guessed he was either very lucky or nobody else knew of his secret place. He wanted it to stay that way because he was rather self-conscious about his particular speciality. People were inclined to laugh at his ears or his bare feet: or both. His ears always had been an obvious problem because they were so large. However long he grew his hair they couldn't really be concealed. His schoolmates were mostly polite about them, but there was always somebody who, on hearing he was a high-jumper, asked with a laugh whether his ears acted like wings to assist his take-off. Invariably that idiot believed he'd cracked an original joke. Sometimes there were variations on the lines of 'Do you have to try and compensate for extra wind resistance?' Steve just tried to shrug off such unkindness but it wasn't easy. The remark might linger for hours.

The bare feet didn't arouse quite so much honour or surprise. After all, most people remembered Zola Budd, the slim, brilliant distance runner who added to her fame by racing without shoes, even on roads and formidable cross-country circuits. Steve preferred to mention in his defence, an international sportsman called C.B. Fry, who had played soccer and cricket for England (once hitting six successive centuries) and had also set a world record for the long jump. Fry discovered it was much easier to jump off a lawn in bare feet than in shoes. Steve, testing out Fry's theory, was delighted to discover that it suited his style, too. So now all his high jumping was done in bare feet, whatever anyone said about it. Sarcasm soon faded away. Success stayed in the mind.

Now he slipped off his trainers and flexed his toes on the damp turf. The feeling was wonderful. He couldn't imagine why all other athletes didn't compete in bare feet. It was so natural, so exciting. He was absolutely certain he'd never jump as well in shoes. It was in his mind this morning that he could break his own record. Until he made a jump he never knew, of course, what height he could manage. But on some days he sensed things were going to go well. This was one of those days, in spite of the dampness of the turf.

Steve had rigged up a line between two wooden sticks in which he'd cut notches at regular intervals; he'd measured the distance between the notches with great care so he knew almost exactly what height he was achieving. True, this apparatus lacked the precision of regulation high-jump poles but it was the best he could manage. And if he was actually jumping *higher* than he ought, well, so much the better.

But, this morning, something about the rope wasn't quite right. For a moment or two he simply stood and stared at it, thoroughly puzzled. Then . . . 'You idiot!' he told himself. 'It's too high – the rope's higher than it should be.' For it was at a height he'd not yet succeeded in clearing. But one thing was certain: he hadn't put it there. So who had?

Steve was agitated. His secret had been discovered: the place he believed belonged entirely and exclusively to him was known to someone else. Known and perhaps *used* by someone else. But that person hadn't destroyed his high-jumping equipment; all he, or she, had done was to raise the level of the rope. But why? As a joke, to see if he could attain that height? If so, then that must mean someone was planning to watch him when he trained.

Instinctively Steve looked round, staring at each bush and tree on the perimeter of the clearing. Was someone even now watching him, waiting to see whether he'd make a complete hash of his jump? Would he hear someone laugh at his failure? Guardedly he went over for a closer look at the densest patch of bushes. He wasn't really surprised to find nothing at all. Probably it was ridiculous to suppose that anyone would turn up so early in the morning to watch him in action.

Deliberately he lowered the rope to the notches representing his second best jump. Probably it was just someone passing who'd noticed the poles and the rope and altered the position for fun: someone with no intention whatsoever of spying on him. It was the spying that worried Steve. It was horrible to feel that someone you couldn't see was taking note of everything you did. Once, in a book, he'd read of a character whose hair began to stand up on the nape of his neck when he sensed he was being watched. Steve now experienced exactly that sensation. But it wasn't going to stop him jumping.

His angled, bouncy, long-striding approach was no different from his usual one: but somehow the usual spring wasn't there. By a deep margin, he failed to clear the rope. He hadn't even managed to equal his second best height. Steve was dismayed. Surely he hadn't lost his touch? As he picked himself up off the ground and re-attached the rope at the same level he couldn't help glancing round again to see whether anyone was watching. Everything, however, seemed perfectly normal and unchanged.

'Come on, Steve, you can *do* it!' he urged himself on as he paused, gathering his strength and settling his stomach, before making the next attempt. Once again he flexed his toes and enjoyed the sensual contact with the spongy turf. He knew he was as fit as he'd ever been; he knew his determination was as great as ever. Therefore he couldn't possibly fail.

But he did.

This time the rope entangled itself with his legs and he crashed quite heavily on to his side. It jarred him so much that for a few moments he didn't even get up. This had never happened before. What on earth was wrong with him?

71

'Was that supposed to be a *real* high jump?' a voice behind him inquired.

Steve's jump to his feet was practically instantaneous; he was so startled his pain was ignored. The boy who faced him was about his own age but, if anything, a little taller. His dark hair seemed to come down as far as his eyebrows and there was an amused expression on his face.

'Who are you? What are you doing *spying* on me?' Steve demanded.

'I wanted to see how good you are,' was the unexpected, frank answer. 'Now I know. You're not much good at all.'

Steve, rattled by this, resorted to time-honoured boasting. 'Course I am. I can jump higher than you any day.'

The other boy just laughed. 'You haven't a hope against me, Crashley. You can't even get as high as your best jump. And your *best* is miles below mine.'

'How d'you know my name? Where're you from?'

'I'm good at finding things out,' the boy told him. He was wearing white shorts, black socks and a tracksuit top. 'I find out who the opposition is and how good they are. Then I know what my target has to be. In your case, it's no contest.'

'Look, who *are* you?' Steve was becoming increasingly nettled. He was certain he'd never seen the boy before and so he couldn't live locally.

'My name's Marcus Muller and I'm going to win the high jump at the Amerton Rival Games,' he replied, looking amused again.

'You can't even enter it! You don't live in the village,' Steve shot back at him.

'My mother does, and that means I have a

residential qualification. I sometimes stay with her so I know what goes on here.'

Steve was taken aback. That was totally unexpected. If Marcus Muller really was an accomplished high-jumper then his own ambitions might be shattered. 'Where do you really live? he asked, trying not to appear too interested.

'In Amerton Magna, of course. The *real* village. Not a – a phoney village like this one.'

But Steve didn't see any point in getting involved in sociological scuffles. 'Are you the person who altered the height of my rope?' Steve asked.

Marcus grinned. 'Of course! I knew you'd never get up to that height. But I thought it'd be funny to see you try. Go on, Crashes. You'll just live up to your name and crash down!'

Steve was fuming but he'd suffered enough taunts over the years about his ears to know it was best not to retaliate. If you ignored insults most people gave up on them and turned to some other subject.

'How did you find this place?' he asked.

'Easy. I was just out for a run one morning, like I am today. I spotted something white moving behind the bushes. So I peered in and saw something terrible – *you*!'

Steve told himself: 'Simmer down, simmer

down. Don't retaliate. Be calm.' So he waited to see what Marcus would say next. And Marcus couldn't resist continuing.

'I think you'd given up jumping for the day, probably failed again. So when I came by yesterday I raised the height to see if you could make it. Of course, I knew you wouldn't. Couldn't even match your own feeble height, could you?'

'Go on, then, let's see what you can do!' Steve challenged him. 'Instead of talking about what you can do, do it!'

Marcus just laughed. 'No, thanks. I'm out for a run this morning and I don't mix my sports when I don't have to. Not during training sessions, anyway.'

'Are you going in for anything else at the Games?' Steve couldn't prevent himself from asking.

'Oh, sure. I'm going to collect a few medals. All top athletes are good at more than one thing, you know. Can you do anything else, Crashes?'

'Naturally,' Steve replied in a deliberately superior manner. He decided that was the way to treat his rival.

'Such as?'

'Oh, you'll have to find out, won't you? When you turn up at the Games, I mean.'

Marcus shrugged. 'Doesn't matter what you

enter. I reckon you won't have much of a tech-nique, judging by the way you do your high jump. Never seen anything quite like it. Right, I'm off. See you.'

Off he went at a speed that took him out of sight before Steve could think of an appropriate reply. It was the criticism of his technique that really bothered him. For all he knew Marcus Muller might be absolutely right in describing it as unusual. Steve hadn't really studied other high jumpers, only having watched them on television. His own style had emerged purely by accident – almost, as he thought of it, a fatal accident. It had saved his life. One or two of his friends knew about it because Steve had told them; but they thought it was hilarious so now he was very cautious about telling others. Not for the world (or a whole fistful of medals) would he have told Marcus Muller.

One day, as he came out of a friend's farm and started to walk home he was set upon by a dog that was foaming at the mouth. He knew that meant the dog could be mad, that it might have rabies; and any bite from such a dog could be fatal. So he ran, ran as fast as he'd ever done in his life. And the dog chased him. A hedge faced him as he raced across a lane and, without hesitation, he jumped it. The dog still pursued him. Steve kept going, took a stone wall in his stride and then, as the dog seemed about to catch him, he leapt into a tree.

A man, who'd seen what was happening, eventually sent the dog away and Steve was able to come down. No, the man explained, the dog wasn't really foaming at the mouth: it'd just been helping itself to some fresh milk from a bucket in the cow shed. That was why it looked as if it had symptoms of madness. It was a very lively dog and if people ran, it gave chase. 'But you weren't in any danger, lad. All the same, that was a champion jump over the hedge. Just in the style of Rival's own champion, Peter Gateway. He jumped to fame, you know, by jumping a great big hedge in the village – that huge hawthorn down in Layton's Lane. You must have heard all about it at school or from somebody.' Steve had, so he nodded, though it would never have occurred to him to link the two feats. 'So if you can jump like that, lad, maybe you ought to think of entering the Olympics yourself.'

After that encouragement, Steve had taken to the high jump and found he was really quite good at it. Not a thought had he ever given to his own *technique*. Now Marcus' comment worried him. *Ought* he to try and improve his style? If he didn't, would Marcus defeat him easily? If that happened, all Steve's dreams of triumph and fame would evaporate like mist when the sun came out.

6

Mr Judge's Verdict

With deep mistrust Kristian Meldrum examined the wound in his leg. By now it was supposed to have healed but, in the purple and the green and the custard yellow of the bruise, he could still detect the puncture marks of Larry's teeth. They looked to Kristian as if they might still open up again into blood-dripping wounds at any moment. Tentatively he squeezed the edges of the damaged area and winced even before he felt a thing.

'You're not *still* poking at that tiny bite, are you?' his mother asked sharply as she came into the room. 'Honestly, you're the most morbid child I've ever heard of. God knows why you had to be mine!'

'I'm not morbid, I'm just examining my injury to see whether it has any chance of healing,' Kristian protested. He knew that morbid had something to do with being fascinated by disease because his mother had accused him of that crime before. Because it was one of her favourite words he'd looked it up. He couldn't imagine why she thought it applied to him.

'You know something?' he grumbled. 'If I'd had those stitches in it then it would be completely better by now. So I wouldn't be worrying myself out of my mind about being fit enough to compete in the Games. I mean, it is the one day in my whole *life* I've planned and worked for like mad. Then that rotten dog has to go and –'

'Now, that's enough Kristian! You know very well Larry would never bite anyone, especially someone in his own family. So you must have been doing something absolutely ghastly for it to happen. And Dr Danzill was perfectly adamant you didn't need a single stitch. You've only yourself to blame if you don't do well in the Games.'

He had always known he'd get no sympathy. No one cared a jot whether he won or lost, lived or died. When she first heard about the biting incident Fiona's only concern was whether her precious labrador had damaged his teeth! 'They are getting a bit loose, you know, because he's an old dog,' she pointed out. There wasn't a scrap of truth in that, of course, but nobody would listen to Kristian's view. Everyone else was full of praise for what Fiona described as Larry's 'heroic' defence of Kristian against the vicious goat (at least they had believed Kristian's story of Gregory's unprovoked attack on them).

He limped up to his room. The limp was only slightly exaggerated (in the vain hope it would raise feelings of guilt in his hard-hearted mother) and he daren't admit even to himself how worried he was about his chances of competing in the cycle race. He sank on to his bed and felt like weeping. All his months of meticulous planning, all his zealous training (yes, over and above his own exacting schedule), all his hopes and determination – all for nothing? All because of a lunatic goat and a dog so daft it couldn't tell friend from foe! Tonight he should have been on one of his final tuning-up spins and confidently looking forward to collecting that gold medal. Instead, he'd ridden no further than the end of the lane. His leg had begun to ache abominably. The doctor had told him to rest the injury as much as possible, promising it would clear up in a week or so if he followed instructions. Well, he'd done his best but he couldn't resist having a brief try on his bike one evening when no one was about.

For the first time since he'd learned to ride, he actually fell off – fell off without being able to save himself. The pain was excruciating when he put pressure on the pedal. He couldn't

understand why it was so bad. After all, he'd been able to walk and even kick a football that crossed his path at school. It had to be because he used different muscles in his leg when cycling – and those were the injured muscles.

He lay back and thought about Games Day: everyone seemed to think it was going to be the greatest day in Amerton Rival's history. Well, perhaps the second if you took into account the day Peter Gateway jumped his way into an Olympic record and put his home village on the map forever. Kristian feared it wasn't going to be his greatest day at all. If he couldn't ride he had nothing in the world to look forward to. His second groan was even louder and Larry, half slumbering on the ground floor, looked up worriedly. The labrador wondered whether there was some dreadful fate in store for him. These days Kristian seemed to him to be a worse enemy than the belligerent bulldog.

At the moment that Kristian was contemplating a dismal future, Susie Linacre was speeding up one of the steep slopes above the village. This time she was travelling not on two feet but on two wheels. In spite of the severity of the gradient she was maintaining an excellent speed. On this form, she told herself, she ought to win the cycle event quite comfortably. Already she had been out on her final training run and she was even more confident about the outcome of the mini-marathon. Her friend, and un-suspecting rival, Lynda Casco hadn't really bothered to train very much; she gave the impression she regarded the result of the race as a foregone conclusion. Not once had she asked Susie if *she* were competing in the Games. So Lynda was in for a shock.

Susie grinned at that thought and then smiled quite brilliantly when she remembered the new outfit she'd bought for the cycle event. The T-shirt was a spectacular yellow and low cut while the pale blue shorts were simply as adequate as they needed to be; the white socks would emphasise the slimness of her ankles. Susie Linacre on a racing cycle couldn't fail to attract every male at the Games. She stood on the pedals and pistoned harder still.

'Wish fussy old Kris could see me now!' she told herself. Then, a few moments later, she revised her thinking. 'Or do I? Won't it be lovely to see the surprise on his miserable face on Saturday?'

Someone else indulging in a secret activity was Hannah Donini. She was keeping out of sight of everyone as she practised her throwing in the small orchard at the back of her home. If her aim with the football was perfectly accurate then the ball bounced back from the trunk of an apple tree. But aim didn't really matter: distance was what counted. And the distance she achieved with some of her throws would have thoroughly impressed any spy watching. Her pony tail swung from side to side as she threw and threw again.

Hannah wasn't really the sporting type. For one thing, she tended to eat rather too much of the family ice-cream. But she was keen to enter at least one event in the Rival Games and being invited to serve on the Committee had simply sharpened her interest. Then, by sheer luck, she remembered she'd once gained kudos by catching a football during one of the boys' matches and instinctively throwing it back. She threw it so hard it almost looped over the far touchline. Some of the boys, and most of the girls present, had laughed about that and then forgotten the incident. A few days later Hannah, who'd been sitting in the garden reading, was hit accidentally by her brother's football; without thinking about it, she'd thrown that back, too – from a sitting position. Thus was born her idea for the competition she suggested to the Committee when they were looking for a replacement for the javelin. She really had no idea whether girls were better than boys at the seated football throw; but saying so had helped to get the idea adopted.

She should have been at the Committee meeting that night but Mr Judge felt it was asking too much to expect her to attend a meeting that might go on very late.

Still, Hannah had found the ideal way of making up for that disappointment. She would refine her throwing technique because everyone else was out of the house that evening. She was determined to win a prize at the Games. Then she would be known for something *she* had achieved instead of just being famous for the family ice-cream.

This time she missed the apple tree but she didn't mind going to retrieve the ball when it had gone as far as *that*!

At the committee meeting in the back room of the Black Bull that evening Kirk Heaton was less than happy with life. In the first place, he'd been re-luctant to use a room that was his favourite drinking spot with his customers; in the second, he'd been over-ruled in his objection that the night immediately before the Games was far too late to make any important changes, if changes were needed.

'Nonsense!' Mr Judge replied pretty pre-dictably. 'We can change anything we like if we want to. Just –'

'You can't change the venue, the village green is the *only* place that's big enough,' Kirk pointed out triumphantly. 'Most of it has already been marked out and –'

'Mr Heaton, please be sensible,' Mr Judge said in a surprisingly mild way. 'If we had to change from the village green the entire Rival Games would have to be abandoned. We *all* recognise that, surely. But there are minor matters that need attending to, I's to be dotted, T's to be crossed, that sort of thing, you know.'

He might have been talking to a child, which was ironic as it was the first meeting at which Hannah Donini was absent. The Chairman knew that tomorrow was going to be one of the finest days of his life since he'd umpired in a Test match at Trent Bridge. He was determined that nothing should spoil it. Not even the facetious Kirk Heaton was going to ruffle his calm approach to Games Day.

'Perhaps,' he said gently, 'we should have a drink to mark this penultimate Committee meeting, penultimate because, of course, there'll have to be another one next week to report on the Day's success and to make provision for distributing any monies left over after meeting expenses. So, Mr Heaton, if you'd be good enough to take orders from everyone. . . . And, naturally, the drinks are my treat. It's a small way of saying thank you to everyone for all *you* have done for the Games.'

There were murmurs of appreciation all round the table; no one declined the Chairman's unexpected offer. Kirk was abashed. He sensed that it would have been better if he himself had offered to provide a free round of drinks. After all, it was his pub and so he was the host. Now C.R. had cleverly out-flanked him and got every other Committee member on his side in the same move. Shaking his head like a bowler who's just suffered a bad decision from an umpire, he picked up a notepad and started to collect orders. It was only later that it occurred to him that he should have summoned a member of his staff to do a job like that; it was what he paid them for.

Eventually, when he sat down after distributing the drinks, he was rewarded with a serene smile from Miss Selby and that cheered him up. They had been asked to judge three of the events together and he looked forward to her company. He'd decided to wear a buttonhole – a carnation, perhaps – for the occasion. So it would only be appropriate to present her with some flowers, too. He guessed she'd appreciate that kind of gift.

'Well, here's to the success of the Rival Games – and to the memory of Peter Gateway in whose honour we are holding them,' the Chairman said, raising his glass high. 'And now we must get down to work. . . .'

So they talked away about the remaining problems. Car parking: 'Mr Watson has said he won't make any objections so long as we put up a notice to say no one must park within two metres of the entrance to his drive.' Programme selling: 'We've got to impress on the sellers that *everyone* must be persuaded to buy one so that we can hope to cover our costs.' The prize-giving company: 'Well, of course, I'll present every one of them if you wish it,' Mr Judge remarked without a hint of a blush on his leathery cheek. Positioning of mobile toilets: 'Mr Watson says he will personally sue every member of the Parish Council and the Games Committee if just one person calls at his house asking to use his personal lavatory.' Raffle prizes: 'People have given us all sorts of junk. Really, who on earth's going to want to win a pair of china rabbits with the ears missing!' The Pets on Parade: 'So, by a majority vote, we agree to stage this event in the interval between the field games,' the Chairman noted.

'I still think it will be looked upon as a de-finite down-grading of the day, having animals on show,' contended the oldest member of the Committee. 'We shall be a laughing-stock everywhere if it gets out that our way of honouring an Olympic Champion was to have poodles on parade! No wonder the TV people are ignoring us. We should be thankful they are.'

The Chairman produced one of his better sniffs. 'The TV people *didn't* ignore us. They merely said they might have difficulty fitting us into their schedule on a busy day of the year.'

'Same thing,' said the objector, stingingly.

'Well, if there's no further business we'll bring the meeting to an end,' the Chairman announced a trifle reluctantly. 'So it only remains for me to wish everyone a very happy and successful Rival Games Day. I'm absolutely certain it will be such a success it will be the talk of the county for many, many years to come.'

'It will be if it's a complete flop, an utter disaster,' the oldest Committee member muttered darkly. 'Then nobody will have a good word to say for it, or for those who organised it.'

But the Chairman didn't hear that. He'd opened the door and great sounds of merriment from the public bar wafted in. Mr Judge smiled. He genuinely liked to hear people enjoying themselves, just as long as it wasn't at his expense. In his mind there wasn't any doubt at all that the villagers of Amerton Rival were going to enjoy themselves hugely the next day.

'Look,' exclaimed Elin excitedly, 'what do you think of this trick?'

She placed Hoovie the hamster on a rubber ball and stepped back to admire his performance. But after one frenzied attempt to get the ball moving under his feet Hoovie fell off and scurried away under an armchair in the Drayton sitting-room.

'Not much,' said Kerry dolefully. She was getting thoroughly fed up with Elin's loony ideas of what her hamster could accomplish.

'But he is getting the hang of it,' Elin insisted as she scrabbled under the chair to retrieve the elusive hamster. 'He just needs more practice and he'll be perfect.'

'Oh yeah,' Kerry commented disbelievingly. 'Look, he can do his spaceship rolling act, so why bother with anything else? I mean, what's the point?'

'The point is,' explained Elin, still trying to corral the creature, 'that when Hoovie wins his event he'll be expected to do an encore – you know, another trick as a celebration. 'So –'

'Yeah, Elin, I do know what *encore* means,' her friend said sourly. 'But, honestly, there won't be time for that. It'll be difficult enough fitting everything in as it is. That's what my uncle says and he should know because he's writing and printing the programme. In fact, it must be finished by now.'

'Ah, got you, Hoovie! You're a naughty boy, a *very* bad boy.' Elin was hugging the hamster with such zeal that Kerry thought she might even squeeze him to death. If that happened, Kerry wouldn't be among the mourners. She'd had enough of Hoovie long ago.

'Now, this time you've got to get it *right*,' Elin went on, oblivious of her friend's intolerance. She placed the furry creature on the ball and, more by luck than anything else, Hoovie succeeded in propelling it a few rolls across the carpet.

Elin was ecstatic. 'You see, he's terrific! I *told* you he was an ace performer. Oh, Hoovie darling, you're going to win top prize as Performing Animal of the Year. No doubt about it. Isn't he, Kerry?'

Kerry had switched on the television and was curling up on the sofa. She would have gone home if only she hadn't promised to stay for supper; and whatever faults Elin's mother possessed, her cooking wasn't one of them. She made the most scrumptious fruit pies – and apricot pie was what Kerry had been offered. It was irresistible.

'Kerry, I asked you a question. Don't be so rude. I want an answer.'

Kerry shot her a glance. There was no doubt about it: Elin had changed in the last few weeks, becoming bolder and altogether less clinging; becoming almost independent. It was amazing what one letter of approval from the Chairman of the Rival Games Committee could do. Certainly that letter about the decision to include animals in the Games had just about changed Elin's life. It had given it a purpose it never previously possessed.

'Well, I wouldn't bet on it, Elin,' Kerry said slowly. She kept looking at the TV set so she wouldn't grin in a give-away fashion. 'I can think of at least one animal that might rival Hoovie. Hey, get that! *Rival* – you know, Amerton Rival and –'

'You're making it up!' Elin challenged. 'You don't know anyone who's got an animal half as clever as Hoovie!'

'Yes I do. I've got a friend with a cat that can – can turn somersaults when she calls out "Pilchards!" That's its favourite food and it'll do anything to get at pilchards, especially in tomato sauce!'

Elin didn't know what to say. The story could be a complete fabrication; it was just like Kerry to make jokes about something really serious. On the other hand, the detail about the tomato sauce sounded convincing. Cats were peculiar creatures.

'You're making it up,' Elin said again, unable

to think of a more damaging comment. 'There isn't such a cat and you haven't got such a friend.'

Kerry did a rather expressive shrug and also produced an enigmatic half-smile.

'Well,' she said calmly, 'you'll find out tomorrow whether it's true or not, won't you?'

7

In the Dark

 Perched on a make-shift stand of a couple of orange boxes, Steve Crashley was studying a garden through his binoculars. It wasn't actually the garden he was looking at, but anyone watching *him* would have been startled by the intensity of his gaze. So far he'd seen nothing of interest but that wasn't going to deter him from keeping his vigil, keeping it until nightfall if necessary.

'He's got to be there, he's got to be!' he told himself.

But there was no evidence at all that Marcus Muller was staying at his mother's home in Amerton Rival on the night before the Games. Following the surprise encounter with Marcus at his training spot Steve had made meticulous inquiries in the village and learned that Mrs Muller did live there and was from time to time visited by her son (though Mr Exley, the Storehouse owner, revealed that the visits weren't frequent, if Mrs Muller's food-buying habits were any guide). Having been spied upon

himself, Steve was keen to turn the tables and get a good look at what Marcus could do. Steve was certain that anyone who was serious about winning the high-jump would put in some practice the night before the competition and would want to be on the spot for an early start.

It was worrying, not knowing how good the opposition was. He'd seen most of the other entrants in action at his own school and was confident he could beat them. But Marcus, with his superior manner, might be anything; he might easily be bluffing.

Then, at last, he spotted a movement in the garden. A woman appeared at the corner of the house. Dressed in a spotted leotard, she wasn't wearing anything on her feet, something that immediately struck a chord with Steve. She was probably a few years older than his mother and, to put it mildly, she was built on generous lines, as the leotard revealed. It was a moment or two before he realised she was launching herself into an aerobics exercise; his first thought was that she was a bit nutty and doing a strange routine on her lawn (if it was her house, that is). Then he noticed the earphones clamped into place and wires leading to a cassette player attached to a waist belt.

Was this Marcus' mother? He had no way of knowing and he could hardly trot over and ask her. She did look funny, doing that weird shuffling and jumping, all on her own, throwing her arms around like a demented swimmer. Steve experienced pangs of guilt because he knew she would hate it if she thought she were being observed. With some apprehension he glanced round, hoping that no one was watching *him*. If they were he might be in real trouble.

Steve lowered his binoculars and stealthily gathered up the boxes he'd been standing on; so he was no nearer knowing whether he would face a formidable rival the next day after all. Still, if he could beat his own record height – and he'd been practising non-stop for days – he believed he had every chance of winning first prize whatever the mysterious Marcus might manage. 'Confidence,' he told himself quite loudly as he turned into the lane leading to his home, 'is worth a head start to every determined athlete.' It was his own motto. And it was true.

'I'll bet you lot any money you like – go on, throw down a tenner and I'll cover it – I will – any money you like. Pete and me will lick you lot into next week.'

Mal Watkins, and the drink, were talking: shouting, really, as Mal and his pal Pete rolled out of the Black Bull after closing time. Mal was in a mood to challenge anyone and all the talk in the bar about the Rival Games had inflamed his ambitions. It was the three-legged race that gripped his mind (it would be unrealistic to call it his imagination). He could win that, he knew, without even trying, it was so simple, boyo.

'Come on then, NOW, not tomorrow, NOW.' He hurled the invitation at Bentley and Nigel. 'You two stick together like twins so let's see how good you are when your legs are *tied* together. Go on, then, show us.'

Nigel would have crept home to his mother if he could but Bentley had also had too much to drink and he wasn't a man to lose face.

'Give us that twine in your pocket,' Bentley demanded, holding out his hand to Nigel, a devoted gardener and therefore sure to have some on him. Nigel handed it over without a word. It never occurred to him to refuse his best friend anything.

With a little difficulty, because his hands weren't exactly steady, Bentley set about tying together Mal's left leg and Pete's right. Then, of course, it was Mal's turn to do the tying and he managed rather better so that Nigel was soon complaining that the twine was slicing his shin off.

'The biggest pain you'll suffer, Nige, is from defeat,' Mal guffawed. 'You'll not beat me and Pete, boyo, try as hard as you like. Right, first to yonder yew tree!'

'You'll wake 'em all up on the other side of the green – old Watson'll go stark raving bonkers,' Pete pointed out.

'It'll be good for 'em, then they'll come out and see some *real* athletes, not the knockabouts that'll be performing tomorrow. Look, are you lot ready?'

With unsteady gait they managed to get more or less into line, Mal insisting he would give the signal to start by shouting 'GO!' at the top of his voice, naturally. Bentley, suspecting that their opponents would steal an advantage by starting a fraction ahead of the signal, paused only a second or two before urging Nigel into motion. Nigel, always eager to co-operate as long as he had warning of what was wanted, didn't react quickly enough. The pair stumbled and then collapsed in a heap.

By now other tardy types leaving the Black Bull and seeing the entertainment being provided gave a hearty cheer. Mal and Pete surged forward simultaneously on Mal's frenzied call. In Mal's view, there was no such thing as a false start: folk either got off when they should have done, or they didn't. His only thought was to win and collect their winnings.

In spite of the liquor they'd consumed, Mal and Pete managed to set up a neat rhythm. Inevitably, they faltered once or twice and there was a moment when Pete had to grab his partner round the shoulders to save him from tumbling into the ancient horse-trough that was one of Amerton Rival's most prized possessions (it was something Amerton Magna did not have). Mal, as was his nature, became over-confident in sight of the winning post. He was clasping his hands above his head in anticipation of giving a victor's salute when Pete, tripping over a loose stone, fell sideways and brought Mal down on top of him.

'Yer great clumsy oafs, yer no good at all!' a spectator yelled derisively. 'Get to bed and sleep it off.'

Pete, having taken a knee in his stomach, was winded and Mal wanted to fight but the sight of their opponents advancing on them restored their active partnership. And their three-legged harmony. As the yew trees loomed ahead of them they even managed a kind of triumphant gallop. The encouragement of some spectators was to Mal like a drink in a desert to a parched traveller. As they crossed the invisible finishing line he felt refreshed enough to run the entire race again.

'Give us the money, boyos, we've won it fair and square,' he demanded as Bentley dragged his sagging partner over the line. And Bentley, too jaded to argue, handed over a couple of notes. He'd collect Nigel's contribution later.

'We've got to celebrate, celebrate like champions!' Mal roared. Pete, groaning, said he was going home, that's how he'd celebrate. Mal saw no value in trying to detain him. 'Tell you what, I'll prove I'm the fittest man in all the Amertons. I'll prove I'm as good as the best there's ever been. I'll prove I'm as good as old Pete any day.'

It was a moment or two before most spectators realised that Watkins was referring not to his now detached partner but to Amerton Rival's most famous son. But they didn't realise that even a drunkard would attempt to do what no other man since Gateway himself had done: jump over the hawthorn hedge in Layton's Lane. Even if you were in perfect physical condition it would be madness to try it. But Mal was the sort of man who believed you needed to be a little mad to get the best out of life.

A few, shaking their heads at such stupidity, went home to their beds; the rest decided they might as well see what a real fool Mal could make of himself. And Mal, puffed up with beer fumes and pride in his latest achievement, was convinced he was a conquering hero as they all turned into Layton's Lane.

It was a lost cause even before Mal made his first run. In spite of its annual trimming the famed hedge was still well over six feet in height and, what made matters still more difficult, it bulged in the middle like a pregnant lady. Gateway, dubbed by the popular newspapers of the day 'The Soaraway Sailor', had been at the peak of his ability when he jumped it in his young manhood; now, even he would have found it an impossible obstacle. On top of everything else, it was barely light enough to see the proper outlines of the hedge for the moon was appearing only fitfully.

'Give it up, lad, you haven't a hope,' an observer advised Mal, now divesting himself of trousers as well as his sweater. 'You'll do yourself a power of damage if you try it. Permanent damage I shouldn't wonder.'

There were murmurs of assent but Mal needed only one voice in his favour, and he heard that soon enough. There are always those ready to provoke others to disaster while standing clear of it themselves.

Even without the drink sloshing about inside him Watkins would probably not have risen above half the height of the Olympic Hedge. To his credit, he got higher than anyone else present would have managed. His run was determined but rather too long. So he was losing speed, instead of reaching a peak, when he took off.

It was his belly that made contact with the swell of the hedge. Despairingly, he flung up his hands in the hope, the foolish hope, of clinging on. Foolish because he suffered deep and painful scratches along the length of his arms as well as on his knees and thighs. Then, like a sack of wet washing, he flopped to the ground. Winded and painfully conscious of his failure, Mal Watkins didn't get to his feet until Pete rushed to help him upright.

'Great try, Mal, great try!' Pete assured him untruthfully.

'Just looked ridiculous to me,' said the observer who'd tried to stop the attempt. 'It's amazing how daft some folk are. Must be a bit of moon madness. Seems to affect some of those refugees from Wales.'

'Tell you one thing,' said another. 'If we don't see some better athletes in action tomorrow, the Rival Games'll be as big a flop as Mal Watkins bouncing off that hedge!'

8

Unexpected Triumphs

Kristian didn't think he could possibly enjoy breakfast on what he hoped would be the most memorable day of his life. He'd looked forward to the day so much he could hardly wait for the Amerton Rival Games to begin. In his opinion, they should have started at 8 am, not 10.30.

'I don't know what you're going on about,' his sister Fiona remarked carelessly as she took her place at the kitchen breakfast bar. 'I mean, you said you wouldn't be fit enough to ride, anyway. I imagined you'd just stay in bed, sulking under the duvet.'

'I'm going to put myself through the pain barrier,' Kristian told her with deep seriousness. 'I know I'm going to suffer but that doesn't matter. This is my chance of a lifetime and I'm going to do my best. Don't suppose I'll win but . . .'

He wouldn't admit, even to himself, that he still had hopes of winning the cycle race. Only forty-eight hours ago the deadly injury had looked as bad as ever and was no less painful; then, in a desperate measure, he'd plastered pure honey on the wound and kept it there under a bandage all night. It was a remedy Mr Exley had recommended: 'I can tell you, young Kristian, that pure honey is a great healer on the outside as well as on the inside of the body.' Naturally, Kristian's mother had been aghast when she heard about it, insisting that it was simply another cunning trick by the shopkeeper to sell expensive foods. Kristian didn't care about that when, the next morning, he un- wound the bandage and discovered his leg looked almost undamaged. The overnight im- provement was almost miraculous. He'd gone off for a ride immediately and once a feeling of some stiffness had worn off there was hardly any pain at all.

His hopes rocketed: but he still daren't think too much about the chances of victory. After all, he'd missed vital training, wasting his time sitting around and chucking a football to a friend who wanted to practise his skills for the football throwing contest, which even Kristian had entered in order to give himself something to do when he wasn't competing in the cycle race, as he'd feared would be the case.

'I'll tell you what,' declared Mrs Meldrum menacingly as she arrived with a fresh pot of tea.

'That honey's not lasted five minutes. Have you been giving it to Larry, Fiona?'

'Of course I haven't!' her daughter protested indignantly. 'Though he deserves a treat if anyone does after the way Kristian's been so rotten to him.'

'Oh yes, blame me, blame me for everything, everyone else does,' Kristian said in the tone of a martyr. 'Anyway, I'm off. Got to put in a bit of practice before the race. Oh, and they'll probably need a hand on the green getting something ready. So you can wish me luck if you like.'

'You'll need more than luck to get anywhere in your race from what I've seen,' Fiona muttered darkly. But only her mother heard that remark and she wasn't interested in what lay behind it. Kristian had already launched himself into action.

In what he regarded as his favourite and most colourful blazer (scarlet and pale blue stripes), and an ancient but well-preserved panama hat, C.R. Judge strolled like the landowner, admiring almost without reservation the bunting and the banners, the white lines of the running track and the floral displays. Amerton Rival, he was sure, had never looked lovelier in its entire history that was said to reach back to Norman times. He felt he could take a little

106

personal pride in what had been achieved in preparation for this historic day. *At least* a little. . . .

'You look pleased with yourself, C.R.,' remarked Miss Selby as she came towards him from the Village Storehouse where she'd been treating herself to some enamel ear-rings in the form of the Olympic symbol of linked circles.

'Every reason to be, my dear,' he replied with a beaming smile. 'Today's what we have all been working for, isn't it? And it's arrived safely.'

'*Safely?*'

'Safely. By which I mean, nothing dreadful has happened overnight. No vandalism, no reports of trouble in the village, drunken stupors, that sort of thing. Why, even the sun is threatening to emerge. Our Great Day is being blessed from above.'

Miss Selby raised her admired eyebrows (admired especially by Mr Heaton, now approaching jauntily). The old boy was rather overdoing it, she thought. But then, she supposed he would never have another day of such importance in his life: Festival Chairman and Chief Adjudicator. Impressive by any standards.

'The hat, I must say, is a delight – very fetching,' commented Kirk as he reached his fellow Committee members. 'Quite a treat these days to see a lady in a *real* hat.'

'Why, thank you, Kirk!' Miss Selby was naturally pleased that someone was being so complimentary; but it also made her wonder whether the hat was being praised because the ear-rings weren't approved of. She herself wasn't sure whether they were a trifle garish for someone in her position. But the truth was she thought she could get away with something garish today. After all, it was supposed to be a festive occasion, a time for enjoying oneself. C.R.'s blazer came pretty much into the same category, in her view. Garish? Yes, it was. But did it matter?

In a variety of moods the rest of the Committee joined them, with everyone vying with one another to pay extravagant compliments to Hannah on her undeniably pretty azure dress. Hannah was wearing it only for the official photograph at the ceremony: after that she wanted to get into her shorts and T-shirt as fast as possible and compete in the event she hoped to win. With due solemnity they all made their way to the Olympic hedge.

'Wouldn't you just know it!' exclaimed Mrs Kenton, picking out from among the lower branches a brown beer bottle. 'Some people have no respect for *anything*.'

'Empty, I suppose,' said Kirk without hope that it wouldn't be.

'No thanks to you – you sold it, I expect,' said Mr Judge with a sudden return to his sharper manner. But then, he was addressing Mr Kirk Heaton.

'You don't think somebody's been trying to *climb* the hedge, do you?' Miss Selby asked, not only in order to restore a friendlier atmosphere. 'I mean, it does look a bit, well, *threadbare*. As if someone's been hitting it with a big stick!'

The Chairman of the Games and Festival Committee, however, was not prepared to discuss such a mundane matter on such a significant day. They had come to honour the memory of the Great Athlete and that they would do. So, in appropriately solemn tones, he read a prepared statement for the benefit of the waiting Press, which actually consisted of just one reporter from the County Printers who wasn't at all pleased not to be given a hand-out. There had been no hand-out. C.R. Judge didn't believe in spoon-feeding people, he said. That was why, five days later, when the report appeared in the *Amertons and District Weekly Star*, the Chairman's speech had been reduced to just one sentence. No one mentioned the regrettable absence of any TV cameramen.

'Right,' Mr Judge concluded, when everybody had had a chance to applaud his oration, 'I think it's time to get on with the main business of the day. So let's go and declare the Rival Games officially open. Let's go and watch people *enjoy* themselves. . . .'

They paraded, the competitors and officials, in their brightest, smartest attire and those who wore, in honour of the occasion, head-bands of laurel leaves, began to experience the feeling that they were taking part in an event they'd remember all their lives. The music for the march came over the public-address system – soon to be taken over for all official announcements by Kirk Heaton, a role which delighted him and worried the Chairman – and, as someone remarked, it was a pity they hadn't a real live band for the day. There had been an offer from one inhabitant of Amerton Rival to provide live music but it had been summarily rejected by the Committee. The offer came from a retired Scotsman who still practised the bagpipes: practised them because he'd never succeeded in mastering them.

They circled the green to sporadic clapping from thin ranks of spectators, thin because most of the villagers had been inveigled into either taking part in the Games or officiating in some way. Hardly anyone had come from Amerton Magna: for one thing, they hadn't been invited, for another they all

maintained they wouldn't be seen dead in neighbouring Rival. At the head of the marchers was the torch-bearer. The flame was rather higher than was advisable and the wind, though hardly strong, was bending that flame closer and closer to the bearer's nose. But he'd been given exact instructions about the angle and height at which the torch was to be held; rigidly, he was sticking to those orders. Which meant he was in dire danger of competing in his chosen event with a scorched nose. But he would regard that, if he won, as a scar of victory.

There'd been some criticism of the running order of the programme but everyone was agreed that it should start and end on a high note: which is why the high jump was the finale and the sprints opened the proceedings. Some had argued that the family tripod should have come first because that involved different age-groups and lots of people who weren't competing in anything else; traditionalists, however, ruled that the tripod was just a 'fun' event and so couldn't be taken seriously. The common belief that the Amerton Rival Games were supposed to be just an entertainment was dismissed by Mr Judge and his closest cronies as frivolous.

Elin Drayton, with Hoovie caressingly clutched in both hands and his spacemachine carried in a plastic bag, impatiently waited for the 'Animals on Parade' event which wasn't scheduled until what the official programme described as the luncheon interval. Nobody had told her that none of the entrants was expected to do anything more than look pretty or well-groomed or generally be no sort of nuisance to anyone, the Committee having decided at a late hour that a class for 'performing' animals wasn't really in keeping with Olympic ideals. However, they had relented to the extent of allowing a Pets Parade to take place and prizes would be awarded for what were vaguely described as 'the most attractive entrants'. So Hoovie's endeavours in his self-propelled module would be in vain, something that wouldn't bother him too much but which might well cause Elin to sink into a morass of tears. Meanwhile, she was able to offer Kerry her usual enthusiastic support for the long jump, one of the earlier events.

Kerry drew many appreciative comments from male spectators as she stripped off her tracksuit. Being Kerry, she was incapable of indifference to such admiration but it was the judge's eye she wanted to catch. Most of the men seemed to think she was just there to show off – and so her style and determination as she flowed down the runway was deeply impressive to watch. Her leap was perfectly timed, her dark, wavy hair bouncing high off her shoulders as she became airborne and provided an amateur cameraman with one of the gems of his forthcoming collection of pictures from the Games.

It was, by her own standard, a magnificent jump, quite easily the very best she'd achieved. No one, apart from Elin, knew just how much effort Kerry had put into her regular training sessions. Now all that keenness paid off. That first jump wasn't matched, let alone bettered, by anyone. Even Kerry herself couldn't equal it when she tried again, as she was entitled to do under the rules of the competition.

'That was great, just great, Kerry!' Elin gushed, flinging her arms round her friend (but only after first carefully placing Hoovie and his space bubble in a safe place). 'I never thought you'd win so, so *easily*. I mean, you were *miles* ahead of everyone else.'

'That's because I set myself the biggest target I could think of,' Kerry explained. 'I didn't tell even *you* that I was getting such a distance. You see, if you don't think big you'll end up as an under-achiever!'

Elin was too excited by all that was happening to ask where that phrase had come from. She had just caught sight of someone who looked distinctly interesting, someone who was actually staring at her with unconcealed concentration, a boy with thin features, dark eyes and a rather confident manner.

As she'd never seen him before she wasn't to know he was Marcus Muller, Steve Crashley's supposed rival in the high jump and part-time resident in Amerton Rival. Marcus wasn't the sort of boy to fall for the all too obvious charms of a girl like Kerry: he preferred the secretive type with hidden depths, which is what he suspected Elin possessed. In fact, he was studying almost a mirror image of himself.

'What do you think *he* is here for?' Elin whispered to her friend, trying to indicate with swivels of her head and eyes who she was talking about.

'Looks a drip to me – perhaps he plays water polo,' Kerry replied so crushingly that Elin never said another word about Marcus Muller to anyone that day; and Elin certainly never told her friend about the 'accidental' encounter after the Parade of Pets when Marcus, with impeccable timing, came up to admire Hoovie in his plastic container. Marcus, it turned out, had a hamster of his own, and Elin was ecstatic to hear it. Kerry, rapidly picking up a posse of admirers from all over the village after her triumph, was happy that at last Elin had found someone else to latch on to for true friendship. Hoovie hadn't won a prize but perhaps Elin had.

As the temperature began to rise, so did the sales of Donini's Gold Medal ice-cream. C.R. Judge, turning a beaming smile in all directions like a lighthouse and accepting compliments on his spectacular blazer, was thinking that it might have been an idea after all to charge for admission in spite of the fact that the green wasn't even enclosed; but the Committee had decided that the Games were for pleasure, not profit. However, a few never-miss-a-chance

115

salesmen had turned up to sell hot dogs and crisps and arty-crafty objects. Mr Exley didn't really mind: he could see that there was nothing of any quality to compare with his merchandise: and, after all, he had the contract for the medals, other prizes and all official souvenirs and a few unofficial ones.

The football-throwing contest was hardly a traditional athletic contest, yet it was very popular, judging by the number of entrants. It was also appealing to spectators who lined the low white-painted rail behind the throwers to shout encouragement and marvel at the various styles and techniques. Some of the throwers lacked any co-ordinaton at all: they released the ball while still preparing to throw. So the ball shot upwards, practically vertically. Others had never worked out what they were trying to do and sometimes the ball went sideways, one even hitting another competitor on the back of the head. But Hannah threw accurately and en-thusiastically – and far!

Her first throw reached the furthest point at which any of the markers was standing. It was her suppleness that gave her such an advantage for, with the ball held by her fingertips, she lifted herself from an almost horizontal position without effort and threw at the precise moment she reached an upright position.

'That's terrific, you're a natural,' Mr Heaton, now superintending this event as a break from loud-speaking, told her. Hannah was delighted.

To the astonishment of the boys, who outnumbered the girls in this game, it was another girl, Justine Browne, who achieved the second best throw of the first round (and each competitor was allowed three throws with the best to count in the final placings). In third place was Kristian Meldrum.

'If you can throw as far as that, Kristian, you ought to take Larry out for walks more often,' his sister Fiona told him. 'You know he loves it when someone throws a stick for him to fetch.'

Kristian wasn't listening to her. Because he wasn't a footballer he hadn't expected to do well in this competition; he'd entered it only to pass the time if he wasn't in the cycle race. Now that his injury had cleared up so miraculously, however, he was feeling in irresistible form. And that undoubtedly helped his throwing. But he didn't want to be beaten by a couple of girls: so he was going to have to exert himself to outthrow them.

On the second round of throws Hannah was unable to match her first throw and her confidence slumped (Miss Selby could have told her she was easily affected by any little setbacks).

Justine improved on her first throw by just a

few millimetres but Kristian, as determined now to win as he was when he rode a bike, put still more effort into his throw. And he was rewarded by cheers from the spectators when they saw he had set a record distance. The school football captain, who happened to be watching, made a mental note to check on Kristian Meldrum's other skills at the game; he would undoubtedly be useful just for taking throw-ins aimed at the penalty area.

'Go on, Kristian, you can do it!' Fiona urged, to her brother's amazement. He never expected support from her for anything he did; but then he didn't realise that, where public events were concerned, Fiona felt the family's honour to be at stake.

Hannah, dismayed to be overtaken by an outsider (as she regarded Kristian) failed dismally with her third throw and dropped out of contention.

This time Justine, a strongly-built girl who played a lot of soccer, often as a goalkeeper, let the ball slip out of her grasp just as she was tensing herself for a superhuman effort. And the rules of the competition didn't allow for extra shots for competitors who suffered bad luck. So, with none of the regular soccer players managing to improve on their previous scores, Kristian was declared the winner without having to throw again.

'Great, never thought I'd do it!' he told everyone who'd listen until Fiona pointed out he was making an idiot of himself and therefore letting the family down (which meant, of course, Fiona). But she revived when she learned what his prize was.

'A whole year's supply of free ice-cream!'

Kristian really didn't know whether he should be delighted or not: he wasn't, in fact, devoted to ice-cream, considering it was fattening for a true sportsman's diet.

'Well, it'll please Mum,' Fiona pointed out. 'She won't have to spend so much money on puddings at the Storeouse. We'll all be able – '

'But it's *my* prize!' Kristian reminded her.

'That's what you think!' Fiona retaliated. 'In our family we *share* success, and don't you forget it. You keep failure to yourself.'

Hannah was feeling a trifle less upset about her defeat now she'd discovered what the prize was ('You see why we couldn't let *you* win, Hannah,' Kirk had sympathised with her; and she knew he was her friend again). She supposed they'd offered that particular reward because it was her suggestion there should be a football-throwing contest. They hadn't worked out that she was hoping to win it herself.

When it was announced that the cycle race was due to begin in three minutes, Kristian was feeling more confident after that unexpected triumph. His injury, he knew, was a thing of the past: he'd just about forgotten it had ever happened. His training rides, when he'd driven himself through the pain barrier and discovered on the other side he was tougher than he thought, told him he was in prime form. From all he knew about other competitors he was sure there was no one else with his ability or determination. Susie Linacre's presence in the field was a surprise because he recalled how she'd run out of stamina while just jogging on the beach. No doubt she wanted to flaunt herself as usual. Susie seemed to believe that everybody regarded her as the prettiest thing on two shapely legs. Well, Kristian for one didn't.

Susie, however, had every reason to be pleased with herself. Like Kristian, she was already a winner. All her hard work and training to defeat Lynda Casco had paid off. Susie had beaten her easily into second place in the mini-marathon, as the organisers insisted on describing the foot race that was less than two miles from start to finish. Lynda had ability, demonstrated in school sports, but her weakness was that she didn't take her best friend seriously as a competitor. So she paid the penalty of over-confidence when Susie led over every centimetre of the course; whenever Lynda tried to dispute the leadership the determined Susie pulled out a bit more to stay ahead. She had developed her stamina by running much longer distances and that strength was now her greatest asset (in sporting terms, anyway).

Those tactics, going to the front from the start

and letting opponents worry about timing a challenge, were the ones she would employ against Kristian Meldrum. She estimated him to be her chief rival and the sort of boy who wouldn't like being led by a girl. She would enjoy defeating the boy who'd been so mean about giving her a sip of his precious drinking water.

Kristian's nerves were taut as he waited for the starter's signal and he didn't hear Fiona's yells of encouragement. By now the entire village seemed to be present at the Games and the atmosphere was that of a fairground on a Bank Holiday. Wherever you looked, something exciting was happening. 'This is the greatest free show, the most spectacular and colourful event, in the entire history of the ancient village of Amerton Rival'. Francis Exley was composing in his mind the article he'd write for the next parish magazine.

Susie surged ahead of the field as soon as the race started. Her admirers were delighted to see her at the head of affairs and Lynda Casco cheered her on vociferously. Lynda's boasting about her own abilities didn't prevent her from praising others when they deserved it; and she still regarded Susie as her best friend in spite of that defeat in the mini-marathon. Lynda didn't bear grudges.

Kristian had planned to take up a position just behind the leaders and then pounce in the final lap. He'd supposed the pace wouldn't be very hot and he could conserve his energy for the moment he most needed it. But that plan was threatened from the very outset. Susie just went on increasing her lead. Nobody seemed capable of keeping up with her. Kristian, frowning, didn't believe she could maintain such a fearsome pace. On the other hand, she was pulling so far ahead she'd soon be able to take a breather if she felt like it while others struggled to catch up.

The race had captured the imagination of neutral spectators, mostly because the sight of a pretty, long-haired, long-legged blonde leading all the hard-pedalling boys by a widening margin was intoxicating. Applause was building up all the time as the eight riders circled the green and even stallholders doing brisk business at the time paused to watch.

'Get going Kris!' Fiona was yelling at the top of her voice. 'If you don't catch up now you'll lose!'

That message got through just as Kris himself was wondering what he should do. Which was unfortunate, really. Kristian hated being bossed by his sister at any time and her support during the football contest was promptly forgotten when he heard her 'orders'. He decided to delay his challenge. Which was fatal. Susie, still sailing serenely along at the same speed, was sure to win if no one caught her up in the next minute or so. And no one did; no one tried until it was far, far too late. Kristian, when at last it dawned on him that he'd fallen into a trap of his own construction, put his head down and rotated the pedals furiously. But although he passed the other riders he couldn't get within five bike-lengths of the leader.

Susie raised her hands high above her head, punching the air with joy, as she swept across the finishing line without ever once being headed. It was her second all-the-way-victory of the day and now she was Amerton Rival's instant heroine. Even Hannah Donini was eclipsed into second place in popularity, something that had never happened before.

Kristian knew why he'd lost: his injury was at last taking its toll of him and the effort he'd put into winning at football had burned up much of his energy. He wasn't a bit pleased about being second but at least he had a convincing reason for not coming first. That mattered to him. Next time, he vowed, he would change his tactics. Meanwhile, he avoided all contact with Fiona. But she, anyway, didn't want to talk to him now he'd spoilt the family record by losing. He went in search of the ice-cream seller to claim the first instalment of his prize.

'Well played, young man,' was the compliment he received from C.R. Judge, who was passing by that moment and temporarily had forgotten that everyone wasn't playing cricket. The day was filling the Chairman with such joy he was beginning to wish it would never end. He could even smile with genuine warmth at Kirk Heaton, though Kirk was so deeply immersed in conversation with Miss Selby he missed C.R.'s ray of approval.

Mr Judge was actually heading for the high jump – the real thing, that is. Because this event symbolised, in his mind, the real purpose of the Rival Games in paying homage to the memory of the village's Olympic hero, he wanted to witness the success of the new generation. 'Who knows,' he told himself, 'we might discover a new champion who will bring fresh glory to Amerton Rival. That will be our symbol of success.' In fact, C.R. was really rehearsing his speech for the closing ceremony. He'd written some notes the previous night but it would look better if the speech was impromptu.

Because he was so used to checking the attire of players in matches he umpired it didn't take C.R. long to observe that one competitor was barefoot. Was that, he wondered as he blinked several times, against the rules of the competition? But then he remembered that no *official* rules had been laid down for any event. All judges had been told to decide for themselves what was fair and what was unfair.

'Are you sure you will be quite *comfortable* running – er, jumping – without proper footwear?' he inquired of the boy with astonishingly large ears.

'Oh, yes, it's *much* better without shoes,' Steve insisted. 'I can get much higher that way.'

'Well, if you say so,' Mr Judge murmured. The boy was not only keen: he seemed to know what he was doing.

The last of the day's worries had vanished for Steve. He'd feared that Marcus Muller would turn out to be capable of reaching unmatchable heights: and Marcus wasn't even competing. 'I was just winding you up, seeing how you'd take it,' the dark-eyed boy from Amerton Magna admitted with a grin when Steven encountered him deep in discussion with Elin Drayton on the topic of the feeding habits of furry fauna. 'I think you're certain to win, so there's no point in me having a go. Anyway, Elin and I have better things to do.' After that announcement, all that Steve had to worry about was whether officials would allow him to compete in bare feet. Now that obstacle, too, had been removed. His mood was buoyant.

Steve was thrilled to hear his name mentioned as he measured out his run. Alphabetically he headed the list of competitors. It should have been nerve-wracking to jump first but somehow it suited Steve.

'I'm jumping *first* – and I'm going to *finish* first!' he told himself loudly as he launched into action. There was now a sizeable crowd and spectators were quite startled by Steve's self-urgings. No one, though, could doubt his determination.

He cleared the bar with some ease and the applause was louder than anyone had heard all day.

The barefoot boy had suddenly captured the imagination of the village. No one had really noticed him before – well, not as an athlete – although his ears had a certain fame.

Now, it seemed, everyone wanted him to achieve what was so obviously a cherished ambition. Really, it wasn't fair on the other competitors, none of whom got even a tenth of the support given to Steve Crashley, Amerton Rival's unexpected new hero, the boy they wanted to see installed as the true successor to Peter Gateway.

Old ladies as well as his own schoolmates wanted to assure Steve of their belief in him, and Steve, trying to appear nonchalant while scratching one bare toe against the other bare calf, basked in such delicious limelight. Until this moment he thought he had preferred complete anonymity.

With his second jump he cleared the raised bar by a still greater margin and the cheers were now almost deafening. Other competitors, sensing with some inevitability that it just wasn't going to be their day, dropped out quite rapidly. Fate had clearly decreed that the 'poor little lad without any shoes' (as one tearful grannie put it) should be awarded the golden crown of laurel leaves, the most costly, and prestigious, prize of the entire Rival Games.

So Steve's third and final jump was simply a victory roll: and he made the most of it by avoiding

the bar by a good margin. When he came down to earth he did a couple of somersaults for good measure. Then, instinctively, a couple of men (actually, the previous night's intoxicated revellers who'd been in the three-legged race) seized the victor and raised him high on their shoulders. Cameras everywhere were clicking furiously and cheers rang out again and again. Steve knew it was the happiest day of his life. He imagined there would never be another like it. So he was going to enjoy every remaining moment of it.

'A jump for joy, that's what we've just witnessed,' C.R. Judge, using a hand-held microphone, told the crowd. It was, he felt, an inspired phrase. 'And a jump for joy is the way I – and I hope *you*, too – will remember the very first Rival Games. They were staged as a celebration, and this day we have much to celebrate. In young Steve Crashley we have, I believe, discovered a star of the future. He is in the very mould of our original champion, Peter Gateway.'

He paused for the applause and then went on: 'Who we shall discover next time, I have no idea. But of one thing I am certain: there must *be* a next time. The Rival Games *must* continue. I am sure that will be the decision of everyone present today.'

For the first time in his life, Mr C.R. Judge was cheered to the echo by all who had heard him.